"You're making a bad mistake, Melanie."

Jamie went on brusquely. "Ross is no more in love with you than you are with him."

"I know what you want!" Melanie said angrily. There was a charged silence, and she began to feel a peculiar languor.

"Do you?" Jamie asked softly. His head swooped, and the feel of his mouth sent slow waves of pleasure through her body. "Now tell me you've ever kissed him like that," he said, and the words were like a slap in the face.

"Take me home," she said hoarsely, trying to free herself.

"How can I get through to you? Don't you understand—"

"I understand that you hate Ross and you're trying to use me to get back at him." Melanie's voice was shaky. "But it won't work. I'm not going to be used as a weapon."

CHARLOTTE LAMB began to write "because it was one job I could do without having to leave the children." Now writing is her profession. She has had more than forty Harlequin novels published since 1978. "I love to write," she explains, "and it comes very easily to me." She and her family live in a beautiful old home on the Isle of Man, between England and Ireland. Charlotte spends eight hours a day working at her typewriter—and enjoys every minute of it.

Books by Charlotte Lamb

A VIOLATION
SECRETS

HARLEQUIN PRESENTS
762—FOR ADULTS ONLY
772—LOVE GAMES
827—MAN HUNT
842—WHO'S BEEN SLEEPING IN MY BED?
851—SLEEPING DESIRE
874—THE BRIDE SAID NO
898—EXPLOSIVE MEETING
971—HEAT OF THE NIGHT
987—LOVE IN THE DARK
1001—HIDE AND SEEK

HARLEQUIN ROMANCE
2696—KINGFISHER MORNING
2804—THE HERON QUEST

CHARLOTTE LAMB

circle of fate

Harlequin Books

TORONTO • NEW YORK • LONDON
AMSTERDAM • PARIS • SYDNEY • HAMBURG
STOCKHOLM • ATHENS • TOKYO • MILAN

Harlequin Presents first edition November 1987
ISBN 0-373-11025-1

Original hardcover edition published in 1987
by Mills & Boon Limited

CHAPTER ONE

THE doorbell rang as Melanie was closing her case and she straightened, dark blue eyes surprised. Surely that couldn't be Ross already? He had said that he would pick her up at ten. A swift glance at her watch told her that it was barely eight-fifteen. She had just finished packing and hadn't even had breakfast yet.

'Melanie—it's Ross!' Her cousin's voice had a familiar dryness—Liz had been cool towards Ross from their first meeting, but then Liz wasn't the type to go overboard about anyone. It might be her nature, or the job she did, but for as long as Melanie could remember, Liz had kept most people, life itself, at a distance. No doubt a journalist had to keep a neutral stance and Melanie admired her cousin's control and poise; yet at the same time it troubled her.

'I'll be down in a second!' she called back, giving her reflection in the dressing-table mirror a hurried check. Her hair was ruffled; she picked up a brush and ran it over the straight, dark strands which floated to her shoulders. Ross was always immaculate; she felt she ought to look the same, not that he ever said anything about her occasional untidiness, but those calm grey eyes noticed everything. It was odd that Liz didn't like him, because Melanie felt that they had a good deal in common.

She ran downstairs, her heart speeding up as she

saw Ross in the hall, waiting for her, the sunlight streaming through the fanlight above the door touching his smooth fair hair, making it gleam. In spite of the sun, the autumn air was crisp, the wind biting. Ross was wearing an elegant dark cashmere coat over a grey suit. Melanie frowned as she noticed that—he wasn't dressed for a weekend in the country, surely?

'You're early—why are you wearing a suit?' she asked as she stood on tiptoe to kiss him.

His pale head bent to meet hers; his mouth fleetingly touched her lips, without passion, without much feeling of any kind, she thought, frowning.

'I'm sorry, Melanie. I can't make this trip to the Lakes. There's been an emergency in Bahrain and I have to fly out there today to deal with it.' His voice was deep, urgent; it was obvious that his mind was already elsewhere and he was in a hurry to deal with the problem of Melanie before rushing off to Bahrain. Yet again she was an interruption in his busy life and he was pushing her aside.

A flush of hurt and anger ran up her fine-boned face. 'Ross, you promised!'

'I know.' He frowned, his mouth impatient. His features had an incisive quality, even when he smiled. When he frowned, as he was doing now, she only saw coldness, remoteness, in the angularity of the cheekbones, the deep-set grey eyes, the harsh jawline and firm, restrained mouth.

'I wouldn't break our date if it weren't absolutely unavoidable,' he said, looking at her as if she were being unreasonable, and her flush deepened.

'It always is, though, isn't it? We're supposed to be getting married, yet I hardly ever see you. We talked this out last month and you promised me you'd take a weekend off and we'd go away, get away from the office and the phones and find somewhere peaceful to spend some time alone, and now this happens . . .' Melanie didn't find it easy to talk to him like that, her voice was shaking and she was trembling, but she was afraid that if she didn't tell him how she felt it would all build up inside her until something disastrous happened.

'Don't shout, Melanie,' he said in a quiet, cool voice, watching her from a distance even though he was merely a foot away. 'Do you want the whole house to hear you?'

She bit down on her inner lip. Liz had gone back into the dining-room and closed the door before Melanie came downstairs. The family were eating breakfast in there, voices lively as usual, laughing over something Teddy was reading aloud from the newspaper. Her uncle Teddy enjoyed making people laugh; he was a natural clown, physically comic with his short, stout figure and bald head, his saucer-like brown eyes.

'Look,' Ross said, 'this crisis on the site isn't something I can shelve or let anyone else handle. There's too much at stake. I have to deal with it myself, or, believe me, I'd send Martin or Gregory. When I get back, we'll fix something, we'll have a long talk.'

There was a new outburst of laughter from the dining-room, and Melanie winced. They all sounded so cheerful, it jarred. A short time ago she had been cheerful, too, imagining that she would soon be driving away with Ross and able to spend time alone with him at last. There was so much about him she didn't know, so much she had to ask. Sometimes she was frightened because she knew so little about him.

'Ross,' she said huskily, 'our wedding day gets closer all the time and I don't feel I know you well enough. We can't go on like this—I hardly seem to see you.'

He looked at his watch, frowning. 'Melanie, I haven't got time for this discussion, I'm sorry. We'll talk when I get back.'

'You keep saying that, but it never seems to happen!' she said. He didn't seem to understand how she felt. He had so much more self-assurance than she did; he had asked her to marry him within a few weeks of meeting her. Maybe she should have said no, but, swept off her feet by his blind rush, she had said yes, completely dazzled. Since then it seemed to her that she had hardly seen him, and she was getting very nervous about the whole situation.

'I'm sorry,' he said again, with impatience. 'I wish I could get out of this Bahrain trip, but I can't. I'd love to be with you this weekend, but I have a company to run and sooner or later you'll have to understand the way my life works. You say you want to get to know me better. Start with that.' He turned and walked away without a backward glance.

He was opening the door as she suddenly came after him, her eyes pleading. 'Ross, why don't I come with you? We could at least talk on the plane; it's a long flight to Bahrain, isn't it?'

He looked round, his mouth taut and wry. 'It sounds wonderful, but it isn't practical, I'm afraid— I have a mass of papers to read before I get there. I wouldn't have time to talk, even if you came.'

He strode away, a tall man, moving with determination, and she watched, her dark blue eyes bright with anxiety and pain, the autumn wind whipping her black hair backwards over her shoulders. As he slid into the back seat of the white Rolls she realised that he wasn't travelling alone. His secretary was in the car, too. Melanie stared at the older woman's profile, averted from her as Brenda Upfield read the pink pages of the *Financial Times* she held. She should have known that Brenda would be going, too. It wouldn't have worked if Melanie had insisted on making the Bahrain trip; she and Ross would never have been alone.

She shut the door and leaned on it, fighting an outbreak of tears. She couldn't let the family see her crying. She ran a trembling hand over her eyes; her lashes were damp. Thank heavens she wasn't wearing mascara, there would be no betraying streaks to tell the family what had happened.

It was five minutes before she felt calm enough to join them. When she opened the door they were all talking at once, which wasn't unusual. Breakfasts in this house were often sheer chaos.

This morning, though, she got the impression that their chatter and laughter wasn't quite genuine. They were acting. How much of what was being said in the hall had they overheard?

Aunt Dolly immediately poured her some coffee. 'Your kipper's still hot, dear, come and eat it. I'll make some fresh toast.' She was over fifty, not that you'd guess it if you didn't already know, because Dorothy Nesbitt had always looked years younger than her real age. She was exactly the same weight and shape as she had been when Edward Nesbitt first met her, so Uncle Teddy insisted. It was impossible to get out of them a true account of which had first acquired the nicknames by which they had now been known for years. Nobody else remembered. They had been Dolly and Teddy throughout their married life and old snapshots of Aunt Dolly showed her as a girl

with the same curly blonde hair and round baby
blue eyes, the dimples in her cheeks, the sunny
smile. She hadn't aged the way Teddy had—he
had once had auburn hair, he claimed. Now it was
a grey fringe at the back of his bald head, no sign
of red in the few straggling hairs.

Their son, Will, had red hair, so perhaps it was
true. Lanky and cheerful, his mop of orange fuzz
was his most memorable feature. Will's face wasn't
handsome, it wasn't even comic, like his father's.
He had a lugubrious face, in fact, but a far from
mournful nature.

As Melanie sat down in her usual chair, next to
him, he gave her a gentle smile. 'You look fabulous
in that sweater. Blue's your colour, you ought to
wear it more often.'

He was trying to make her feel better. She gave
him a smile that tried hard to be steady. 'It's my
sailing sweater, I've decided. Perfect for sailing,
don't you think?' Then she bent her head to eat
the kipper which had been kept hot under a plate.
It was perfectly cooked, of course, the smoky tang
exactly right and the flesh melting off the bones.
Aunt Dolly was a very good cook and up to
tackling anything from a boiled egg to a cordon
bleu meal.

'Toast coming up.' Will passed the white bone
china toast-rack while Uncle Teddy poured her a
cup of tea, and Liz pushed the white bone china
dish of marmalade towards her. It was the usual
concerted family effort to make her feel happy;
Melanie loved them for it and was angry with
herself for feeling at the same time a prickling
impatience, not with them, but with fate. She
sometimes got so tired of being an object of pity;
that was the last thing she wanted at this moment.
She felt like saying to them: stop feeling sorry for

me, stop being so kind, but how could she? It would hurt their feelings, and she didn't want to do that.

The family team-work had begun when she was thirteen and her parents were killed in a car crash, which left Melanie seriously injured. For six months she had been in and out of hospitals. Her father had been Uncle Teddy's brother. From the minute she was conscious of what was going on around her, after the accident, Uncle Teddy and Aunt Dolly had been at her bedside to reassure her. She had a home with them, they loved and wanted her, everything was going to be all right, they said. Will and Liz welcomed her with open arms. This house was Victorian, large, shabby, with many rooms. When Melanie got out of hospital and came here to live, she found that they had moved every stick of furniture from her old bedroom at home and had a bedroom redecorated for her. Her dolls sat on the bed in which she had always slept, her books were arranged on a shelf, her clothes hung in the same wardrobe. It was sensitive and thoughtful, and she didn't cry until she was alone and they couldn't see.

They wanted so much to help her. Their own lives revolved around that thought. They treated her like precious china and Melanie began to wish that Will would shove her the way he did his sister, that Liz would be sarcastic with her the way she was with Will, that Aunt Dolly would sternly tell her to tidy her room the way she did both her children or Uncle Teddy scowl over her school report and say, 'This isn't good enough!' as he always did to Will, who was more or less the same age.

How could Melanie tell them that their unremitting tenderness towards her made her feel like a victim of tragedy all day? She couldn't forget the way her parents died because the family were so terrified of hurting or upsetting her. She was constantly reminded of the crash.

Gradually, of course, life had become normal, but today Melanie was bleakly aware that they were sorry for her again. The very fact that they hadn't asked any questions or made any comments told her that they had guessed what Ross had come to tell her, and were busy trying to comfort and pet her.

'Look at that time,' Uncle Teddy said, getting up with a last gulp of tea. 'I'd better rush. Want a lift, Will?'

'Thanks, Dad. Will you have time to help me with my bike this weekend? It's still in pieces in the garage.'

'Why did you take it apart if you didn't know how to put it together again?' Uncle Teddy said drily but without heat as he kissed his wife on the top of her silvery blonde head.

Will leapt up; a gawky young man, he plunged about like a nervous horse, his body never quite under his control. 'I thought it would be simple enough,' he explained defensively.

His father grinned. 'Famous last words.' He came round to kiss Melanie's head. 'Have a good day, sweetheart.'

'Hey, why don't we go to the pictures tonight?' suggested Will. 'There's a great film on this week. Want to see it, Liz? You like horror movies. You should, you belong in one.' He skipped out of the way as his sister threw a punch at him. 'Missed me. Yah, yah.' He slammed out of the room after his father, laughing noisily.

'I'm glad he isn't riding that terrible motor-cycle at the moment. I wish it would stay in pieces.

Every time he goes out on it my heart is in my mouth.' Aunt Dolly began clearing the table and Melanie and Liz got up to help her.

'What are you going to do today?' Liz asked a few minutes later as Melanie was going upstairs to her room.

'I'm going to the Lake District,' Melanie said calmly, and felt Liz do a double take.

'Oh.' Liz stood on the bottom step, staring after her, mouth rounded in surprise. She bore no resemblance to any of the rest of the family. Tall, slim, with sleek brown hair and brown eyes, Liz had a face which kept its secrets: calm, smooth-skinned, even-featured. You could rarely tell what Liz was thinking. Even her flashes of sarcasm were carefully controlled. She never exercised them on Melanie.

In her bedroom Melanie lifted her suitcase down and went to the wardrobe to get her anorak. As she knew, it often rained in the Lake District, and it was wisest to be prepared for bad weather, especially in the autumn.

Liz loomed in the doorway. 'I'm in the mood for a little sailing, myself,' she said casually, but not quite casually enough. Melanie heard the thought behind the words and gave a short sigh.

'I'd rather be on my own, Liz, if you don't mind.' She wished Liz hadn't made the oblique offer because she didn't want to offend her. It was kind and thoughtful, but company was the last thing she wanted.

'It isn't a good idea to sail alone,' Liz pointed out gently enough. 'You know the weather can come up suddenly and Ullswater can be pretty rough.'

'I won't take any risks.' Melanie threw her anorak over her arm and picked up her case. She was warmly dressed in the blue sweater and dark blue cord trousers. She was slightly built, a girl who resented her own look of fragility because she didn't feel fragile inside; she wanted to claim an independence and self-sufficiency those around her seemed reluctant to admit. Her outward look betrayed her; those large haunting blue eyes, the long fine black hair, the pale skin and finely shaped features. Inside, she felt much tougher than that. She didn't want to lean or cling, she didn't want to be protected, she had had too much of it in the past, she didn't want Ross to treat her as a plaything, a doll, to be picked up and put down when he hadn't anything more important on his mind.

'It would be fun,' Liz said, faintly wistfully. 'We haven't been to Ullswater for a month.'

The family kept a small sailing boat moored there, had done for years. They lived on the outskirts of Carlisle, only half an hour's drive away, and throughout their teens had spent most of their summers on the lake, sailing, swimming, walking.

'Next time,' Melanie said, almost desperately. She turned and looked at her cousin frankly. 'Liz, please—I have to get away on my own. I have to think.'

Liz shrugged, a mixture of anxiety and wry understanding in her watchful eyes. She was three years older than Melanie, and had always been just that little bit ahead of her. Liz, of all the family, would be most likely to understand Melanie's need to be alone and think, because Liz wasn't given to confidences either. Cool, sophisticated, very sure of herself, she wasn't easy to get to know.

'Don't brood over Ross Ellis. It's time you

realised that he puts his job before everything else,' Liz suddenly broke out. 'He's never going to have time for you. Men don't change, Melanie. Don't hope he will.'

Melanie didn't answer. She walked past her cousin out of the room and down the stairs. Her case wasn't heavy; she had packed very little. She wouldn't need much for a weekend's sailing—denims and shirts and sweaters, one pretty dress for evenings, a change of underclothes.

'You'll be staying at the pub, as usual?' asked Liz, following.

Melanie nodded. 'Say goodbye to Aunt Dolly for me. I'd better be on my way.' She didn't want to go through a session of questions and parried answers with her aunt too.

Her car was old and temperamental. She was terrified that it wouldn't start; on cold mornings it often didn't. She had a routine of taking out the sparking plugs and heating them to get the engine going but she didn't want to be delayed this morning because it would give Aunt Dolly a chance to get at her.

She prayed silently as she pulled out the choke then turned the ignition key. One outraged splutter, then the engine reluctantly fired and she drove off just as Aunt Dolly appeared in the doorway, distraught and flustered in her flowered pinny, waving a delaying arm, her mouth open in a wail of dismay. Melanie waved back without stopping.

It was a Saturday morning; the roads crowded with traffic. People going weekend shopping, people heading for the lakes or the sea. Melanie got on to the motorway and was able to put on more speed. Her old Ford couldn't safely do more than fifty or sixty miles an hour, but even so she was cresting the hill above Ullswater in no time at all, her eyes

delightedly absorbing the landscape. The sky was a
stormy blue, rainwashed but full of light; the green
hills seemed to float in that brilliance like a mirage,
reminiscent of a Tolkien illustration. Watery
sunlight struck across Ullswater, the rippling surface
of the lake shimmering.

The family always stayed at a lakeside pub
owned by people they had known for years.
Melanie turned into the crowded little car-park
and saw just one space left, over by the wall. It
wasn't easy to get into, which was probably why it
was still vacant. She moved forward a little to get
into position to reverse carefully into it, only to
have her engine stall. Muttering under her breath,
Melanie tried to get the car started again. While
she was busy doing that a sleek red sports-car shot
into the car-park, moved behind her and neatly
slotted into the space she had been going to take.
Melanie was too angry to admire the skill of the
driver who performed the manoeuvre swiftly and
without hesitation. Turning red with fury, she
stumbled out of her car and went across to tell him
what she thought of him.

He was just climbing out on the far side near the
wall, his black hair blown around by the wind. He
glanced over his shoulder at her as he bent to lock
his car. His profile had a rakish elegance; sharp
cheekbones, a long, arrogant nose, a rugged
jawline. It was a very memorable face; hardly
handsome yet stamped with a strong personality.

'You've taken my space!' Melanie accused.

'I didn't see a name on it,' he said with
breathtaking insolence, straightening to stare at
her. Seeing him full-face, she realised that it wasn't
the jagged lines of his features that made the most
impression, it was his wild black eyes. She'd never

seen such amazing eyes before, and stared at him for almost a minute in surprise.

It wasn't until he was walking past her that she came to her senses. 'I was just going to park there!' she told him angrily.

He paused beside her, looking amused. 'How was I to know that? Your engine was switched off.'

'It wasn't switched off—it had stalled!'

One brow rose crookedly. 'Oh, was that it? Well, I'm sorry, but I saw an empty space and I got into it. That's the way it is around here. Parking is at a premium. If you see a space you don't wait around, you grab it. You may find somewhere further along the lake if you hurry.'

He turned on his heel and vanished into the pub and Melanie stared after him, bristling. He didn't even care! But there was nothing she could do about it now. She would have to take his advice and go and find somewhere else to park once she had checked into the reception desk and left her suitcase. She drove over to the side of the pub and parked there while she carried her case inside the little lobby. The owner was sitting behind the desk, going over some paperwork and operating the small switchboard.

'Hallo, Fred,' Melanie said, putting down her case, and he looked up, his thin face breaking into a grin.

'Melanie. Hi. I hope you've brought some better weather with you. It's been raining on and off since early morning.' He peered past her. 'Where's your fiancé?'

'He couldn't make it,' she said, hoping she didn't sound too uneasy about that. 'He'll have to come next time.'

'Okay. You'll just be wanting one room, then.'

'I'm sorry, Fred. If you can't let the other one, of course we'll pay for it.'

'Don't worry your head about that—we'll let it! We're turning people away all the time. We get busier every year. Sign in and I'll give you your key.' He pushed a card over to her and she quickly signed her name and address.

'Fred, I couldn't find anywhere to park,' she began, taking the key he held out.

'Give me your car keys and I'll put the car round the back, but don't tell anyone or they'll all want to do the same.' He winked at her. Fred Hill was in his early sixties, grey-haired, fit, with wind-tanned skin and a relaxed manner. He'd once told her that he had worked in a factory in Birmingham for thirty years until he had an accident and had to retire early. He'd invested his life savings in this little pub beside Ullswater. His wife, June, did the cooking and saw to the bedrooms. Fred managed the books and entertained the bar guests. The eight bedrooms were always full, and so was the bar. June's cooking was good. Fred's cheerful smile brought people back again and again. They often wished that Fred had had his accident years sooner; they were happier than they had ever been in their lives.

'Thank you, Fred,' Melanie said, relieved and grateful, and handed him her car keys before she went up to her room. June had put her in the one she always had; a room with a bay window and a view over the lake. It was comfortably but shabbily furnished; an old, faded red Axminster carpet on the squeaky floor-boards, well-washed chintz curtains at the windows, solid Victorian furniture which was always highly polished. There were none of the delights of modern hotels; no television, no telephone in the room, the bathroom was poky and only just held a shower cubicle and lavatory, a tiny wash-basin. But the bed was more than comfortable, the mattress was stuffed with feathers, and sleeping in it was like sinking into a snow drift. The quilt was massive, a faded pink satin. There was no central heating in the pub yet; in winter these rooms were like wind tunnels and the air smelt of damp. You needed a thick quilt. Whatever the season, Melanie always slept well here, especially after she'd been out on the lake or climbing in the hills all day. Fresh air, exercise, good food, made her ready for bed by nine o'clock each night.

She unpacked and changed into her old sailing denims. Before she went downstairs she stood by the window looking over the lake—the water sparkled, the pine trees across the water gave a mysterious edging to the horizon, dark, battlemented. Autumnal colours touched everywhere else; the birches and elms rustled golden leaves and every breath of wind brought new leaves blowing along the water's edge.

Ross would be on his way to Bahrein now. If he loved her, he'd be here. What was she going to do?

She closed her eyes, fighting with new tears, and turned away, refusing to think about it yet. She needed the solace of the silence on the water before she could think without crying.

She ran downstairs and June met her in the lobby, giving her a comfortable hug. 'Hallo, ducks, how are you? Where's your lover boy, then? Not coming, Fred said. Business! You shouldn't let him get away with that, lovey. If they're at it before you're married, they're devils after the knot's tied.'

Melanie forced a smile. 'You know what men are like, June!' she said gaily. 'Anything special for lunch today? I thought I'd have a snack before I went out in the boat.'

'Come in the bar and have some of my shepherd's pie. I've put a cheese topping on it today. One of my better efforts, if I say so myself.' June bustled ahead, plump, gaudily blonde with an easy smile and a genuinely kind heart behind it. Her natural colouring was brunette—you could see the dark roots because she dyed her hair herself—but somehow being blonde suited her far more, it matched her cheerful personality. All the regulars at the pub loved June; she was an instinctive home-maker and enjoyed looking after people.

As Melanie climbed on to a bar stool she saw the man who had snatched her parking space. He was sitting at a table in the corner with a tall red-head in a smart dress. They both looked out of place, for different reasons. This wasn't a 'smart' pub. It was down-to-earth and lively but the jet set didn't congregate around here, and the red-head looked pretty jet set to Melanie. The studs in her ears were real emeralds and she was distinctly wearing a Cartier watch.

Her companion wasn't as easy to place. He had been wearing a sheepskin jacket which he had thrown over a chair. Now Melanie could see that his denims were as old as her own and his sweater was hand-knitted Fair Isle. He was wearing trainers on his feet—no doubt he had been or was about to go sailing, but not with the expensive lady sitting next to him. Her high heels were delicate enough to be hand-made.

'Here you are, ducks. Get that inside you and you'll be fit for anything!' June placed an oval dish of cheese-topped shepherd's pie in front of her. 'Now, what'll you have to drink with it?'

'Let me buy you a drink,' said a voice behind Melanie. 'A small apology.'

'What's that when it's at home? Don't think we've got any,' said June and gave one of her roars of laughter at her own joke. 'Now then, Jamie Knox, what've you been up to? Melanie's a friend of mine. I won't have you upsetting her.'

'He stole my parking place,' Melanie said without looking at him as he slid on to the stool next to her. She remembered his striking face without needing to see it.

'Typical,' June said, leaning her elbows on the counter to enjoy the discussion. 'Watch out that's all he steals—he's a devil with the ladies, aren't you, Jamie?'

'If Fred hadn't seen you first, I'd never stray from your side, June,' he said lightly, and June chuckled.

'Flatterer. Come on, Melanie, what about some champagne on Jamie? Make him pay for his piracy.'

'I'll just have a Perrier, thanks.'

'Don't let him off lightly; that's a mistake with guys like Jamie Knox!'

'I'll need all my wits about me while I'm sailing,' Melanie said coolly, turning her head to meet his dark gaze. June moved away, shrugging, to get the drink, and Jamie Knox smiled into Melanie's wary eyes. He needn't waste that charm on her, she thought, staring back.

'Crewing for someone?' he asked and she shook her head, the sleek dark strands of her hair floating sideways and flicking against his arm. He was sitting far too close for comfort. Melanie found something about him disturbing. She tried to shift away without being too obvious about it. She didn't want him to know the effect he had on her. Those dark eyes were far too aware and cynical.

'I'm going out alone, today,' she told him reluctantly.

His brows shot up. 'What in? A rowboat?'

She stiffened, her colour high. 'Don't be so insulting!'

He grimaced. 'It was, wasn't it? Okay, I apologise—but you look far too ritzy to be the sailing type. Do you really know what you're doing in a boat? What are you going out in? Have you sailed it before?'

'Literally dozens of times—and alone as well as with help,' Melanie said crisply, and he considered her thoughtfully.

'If you want a crew . . .'

'I don't,' she said, before he could offer, trying to sound polite. 'I want to be on my own, thanks.' To make it quite clear to him that she wasn't interested in him, she put up her left hand to brush back her hair and saw his eyes narrow as he noticed her ring. It was hard to miss—Ross had given her an enormous, square-cut sapphire ringed with smaller diamonds. When her hand moved, the stones blazed.

'What about you and your lady-friend, Jamie? Want anything else?' June asked, putting the glass of mineral water in front of Melanie.

'No, I came over to pay the bill,' he said. June told him how much he owed her and he paid, then slid down off the stool and said quietly to Melanie, 'Watch the weather this afternoon; it's very changeable out there.'

Then he was gone and Melanie concentrated on her meal. There was far too much in the oval dish; she apologised to June as she left half of it. 'It's gorgeous, but I can't quite manage all of it, sorry, June.'

'Never mind, ducks. I make my meals man-sized, so I don't expect you to eat all that. Want a coffee?'

'No, I think I'll get out on the water while the sun's out. See you tonight.'

She walked down to the mooring-space in front of the pub, her long black hair whipped around by the strong wind. Good sailing weather, she thought, looking up at the blue sky. Clouds scudded across, driven by that wind, but they weren't rainclouds now. The afternoon was set fair.

As she sailed out from the shore she caught a glimpse of the red sports-car racing along the lakeside road. Ullswater wasn't as swamped with traffic as Windermere, which in the summer was impossible. You couldn't park, or drive faster than a snail's pace, anywhere around Windermere.

She hoped Jamie Knox wasn't staying at the pub too. It wasn't often that Melanie met someone she positively disliked, but she had been left with a far from favourable impression of that man.

The light lasted until well after seven that evening and Melanie stayed out, her body going through the automatic routine of sailing the boat while her mind ran blindly through mazes of doubt and uncertainty about Ross. It all came back to one question—did he love her? If he didn't, why had he proposed? If he did, why did she see so little of him, and when they were together, why did she always feel so strained? When he kissed her it was like being kissed by a stranger, which was what Ross was to her, despite the glitter of his ring on her finger. Was he too old for her? Did he feel that he was? He was thirty-six, Melanie just twenty-two.

Fourteen years, she thought, her heart uneasy. Fourteen years *is* a long time. What do I know about those years of his life? He tells me nothing, and when I try to ask he kisses me to silence me, but making love can't solve everything; and that brought her back to the original problem—did he love her?

That evening she went to bed early after a light snack of salad and an omelette and slept heavily until her alarm clock went off at six-thirty. She had arranged with June to take a packed lunch with her that day. When she got downstairs for breakfast the small morning-room was crowded. Everyone who came here was intent on spending the day in the open air; some were going sailing, others, like Melanie, meant to head for the hills and walk.

There was a faint ground mist as she set out, but the weather forecast had been encouraging. During the morning the mist cleared and the sun came out. At noon Melanie was high above Ullswater on the mountainside. She had climbed up through an oakwood's shadowy glades out into the sunlight on the steep flanks of the mountain, over shifting, jagged stone and short rough grass, pushing herself onwards with an angry need to tire her body and stop her mind working.

She was beginning to be hungry, though, so she stopped, took off her anorak and threw herself down on a patch of coarse tall grass; the purple dancing heads of couch-grass dominating it. Her legs ached and she was out of breath. She unpacked her rucksack and found that June had given her a large slice of cold game pie, a tossed salad in an airtight plastic box, an apple and a flask of coffee. Melanie ate her picnic staring down at the distant gleam of blue water, the ribbon of road, the toy houses and cars around the lake.

When she had finished eating she felt heavy and sleepy. The sun was hot, the grass comfortable.

She only meant to lie down for half an hour before beginning the climb downwards, but she must have been more exhausted than she realised.

The next thing she knew was when a shrill chattering call very close to her woke her. She opened her eyes in time to see a slate-blue merlin chasing downwind with prey in its talons. Melanie was surprised that it came so close to her until she realised that it hadn't seen her. Sitting up in alarm, she realised that mist had come stealing down the mountain while she slept. The lake was no longer visible. The sky was enveloped in damp grey.

Shivering, she got up and put on her anorak, slipped her arms through the straps of her rucksack and began to pick her way carefully downwards. She could still see a few yards ahead of her and so long as she kept going down she must reach the lake in the end, she told herself, but the mist kept getting thicker and the loose stones were slippery and wet now. Her feet kept sliding from under her. She was reduced to moving very slowly, checking each foothold before she risked it, and the longer it took her the less she could see.

Thank heavens she had told June exactly where she was heading! At least her whereabouts would be known if she had to stay put up here. If the mist got much thicker she knew she wouldn't dare risk the descent. The mountains could be treacherous in weather like this. One false step and she could go plunging down to her death.

She had no sooner thought that than her foot skidded on a shifting stone and she felt herself sliding. She clung on to some coarse grass but it couldn't hold her weight. The fall was short, luckily. She found herself sprawling in a narrow gulley. She banged her head but otherwise seemed okay, until she tried to get up. Then she discovered that she had hurt one ankle. Putting any weight on it was painful. She sat down and examined it anxiously; not broken, but already puffing up. She had sprained it, she suspected. This would make her climb downwards even more difficult and dangerous.

It might be wiser to stay where she was until the mist lifted. The sides of the gulley were some protection from the cold. Her anorak was warm, her sweater helped too, and she had a flask of coffee which she had barely touched. June had packed far too much food, as usual. Melanie had been stranded on the hills before now. She knew the drill. Keep warm and take no risks. Sighing, she settled herself more comfortably. She might be in for a long wait—Lakeland weather was unpredictable, this mist might dissolve at any minute, but on the other hand it could set in for hours.

She looked at her watch and was amazed to realise that it was gone four. She must have slept for several hours! Pulling up her hood, she drank a little more coffee; it was still hot and circulated nicely in her chilling body. The mist was very cold, she felt it dewing her lashes as she curled closer to the side of the gulley.

It was some time later that a new sound made her sit up, ears pricked. The sound came again, the rattle of a stone under someone's foot, and then the rough sound of breathing.

Melanie clambered to her feet, wincing as she remembered her swollen ankle. 'Hi!' she called. 'Hi!'

The sounds grew louder, she saw a shape through the mist—a tall, dark shape which materialised as that of a man in a green anorak, the hood hiding his face until he came closer and bent to stare at her.

'There you are,' he said conversationally. 'Not very sensible of you to stay up here with the mist coming down, was it?'

Melanie's heart sank as she recognised Jamie Knox's dry voice. It would be him!

CHAPTER TWO

SHE sank back, her face a battleground, half grateful to see him, half wishing it had been someone else. 'Have you been climbing, too?'

'No, I was having lunch at the pub when the weather warning came at the end of the news. June said she was worried because you were climbing alone.' He dropped lightly into the gulley beside her; she saw drops of mist on his dark hair. 'We took a look through binoculars and thought we saw you right up near the summit, but you weren't moving. June got into a panic, thought you might have hurt yourself, but then we saw you get up and start coming down so I decided to come up and meet you just in case the weather worsened. Just as well I did, isn't it?'

He was still breathing rapidly; he must have climbed fast if he had had lunch at the pub. 'That was very good of you,' she said unevenly. 'I fell asleep, you see.'

'Good God!' he said impatiently, his mouth hard. 'You ought to know better! Falling asleep on the fells—were you trying to get yourself killed? You know how the weather changes around here!'

She bit her inner lip, tempted to snap back, but knowing he was right. It had been very stupid of her to fall asleep, and there was enormous relief in having another human being around in this cold mist.

'It wasn't very bright of me,' she admitted

reluctantly. 'And when I woke up and saw the mist I had to hurry and I slipped and hurt my ankle.' It was best to get the worst out right away, then he could tell her what he thought of her and get it over with.

He gave her one look, charged with feelings she deserved, then knelt down. 'Let me see.' His hands were gentle but she still flinched at the pain of their probing. 'Only sprained,' he said quite soothingly. 'Can you stand on it?'

'Barely.' She had had to unlace her climbing-boot, anyway, which made it dangerous to walk far on these steep slopes.

He stood up and looked away from her, his brow furrowed, as he thought about the situation. 'God knows how long this mist will hang around, and it can be very cold at night up here. We ought to get inside if we can. There's an old shepherd's hut about a quarter of a mile from here on a lower level—if we could reach that we'd be out of the weather. Do you think you could make it if I helped you?'

Melanie tensed her muscles. 'I can try.'

She felt him watching her. 'June says you're used to hill-walking, you know what you're doing, but I'd never have guessed.'

Very flushed, she ignored that. 'I vaguely remember that hut. If we're going to make it before it gets dark, we'd better start now.'

'Let me fix that boot of yours before we move off.' He knelt down again and managed to tie the laces without putting pressure on her swollen foot. 'If you need to lean on me, don't hesitate,' he told her curtly, as they set off.

There was a distinct track running horizontally towards the hut, which was often used by climbers in bad weather. It was easier going than the descent on loose stone, but before they got there it began to rain; thin, driving rain that soaked through her clothes within minutes. Shivering, she paused to wipe her face—she could hardly see a foot ahead now.

Jamie paused, too, looking at her in impatient concern. 'Can you go on? It isn't far now. The sooner we're out of this the better.'

She nodded, her teeth chattering, and Jamie slid an arm around her waist. The track was just wide enough for both of them now but the relentless rain made every step difficult, and just before they got to the hut Melanie stumbled and fell headlong before Jamie could save her.

He lifted her to her feet, his hands under her arms. She leaned on him like a spent swimmer, gasping and shuddering, blood running down her temples where she had grazed her face in the fall, and heard Jamie mutter impatiently, then he hoisted her over his shoulder and carried her the last few yards. She was too weary to argue or fight him. She had never been so tired in her life.

The door creaked as he pushed it open, then they were inside and he kicked the door shut, put her down and produced a torch whose light showed her a bare, stone-floored interior. The hut was primitive, intended only as a shelter from the weather, and it held no furniture. Cobwebs hung dustily from corners, the one window was grimy, straw littered the floor and a set of stone steps led up into a hayloft at one side of the room. Melanie's eyes focused on the wall which held a blackened stone hearth.

'I'll light a fire,' Jamie Knox said, walking away, his torchlight making circles on the floor.

'What with?' Melanie couldn't see any kindling material. She was so cold her body shuddered violently, and she had to lean on the rough stone wall. Local stone, she thought, the same material that had traditionally been used for building drystone walls.

Jamie was up in the hayloft, his feet scuffling in straw. 'They keep a pile of logs up here for these emergencies.' He came down a moment later with his arms full of logs.

'You've been here before,' she said, drawn forward by the idea of a fire. He had knelt down by the hearth and was carefully making a pyramid of straw and pine-cones with logs as the main structure. 'Can I do anything? Get some more logs?' she asked.

'Once I've got this started you can watch it while I bring some bedding down for us,' he said, producing a lighter. Hypnotised, she watched the flame and inhaled the scent of burning resin as the pine-cones blazed up. There was something so primitive about fire; both dangerous and reassuring. Out of control it could kill, but contained within the smoke-blackened chimney it cast a spell, the warmth of it very comforting.

Jamie was crouching down to blow gently upwards; the dry logs caught the flame with a sudden crackle, a fiery tongue licking upwards. 'I'll get the bedding now,' he said, turning to face her on his knees. That was when she realised what he had said the first time, and she reacted with alarm as the firelight flickered, showing her the carved hollows of his face.

Melanie stiffened. 'Bedding?' she repeated guardedly, and his black eyes flashed at her.

'We're going to be here all night, from the look of it out there. I'm not prepared to risk trying to get down in that mist and rain, even if you are.' He got to his feet and she backed, suddenly afraid.

Until then she hadn't really thought about their isolation, but now she was very conscious of it.

He watched her, his features mysterious and sinister in the leaping firelight. Black hair, black eyes, a wilful cast of face—he wasn't the companion she would have picked for a night on the mountain.

'We should be comfortable enough on straw,' he said drily and moved away, taking the torch with him but leaving her in the comforting glow of the firelight. She sat down near it, crouched inside her wet anorak, which began to steam gently. She ought to take it off but she was still cold.

Jamie came back with armfuls of straw and a couple of old sacks. 'These will make useful covers,' he said, laying them down within a safe distance of the fire. 'You'd better take your anorak off or you'll be going down with pneumonia.'

She unzipped the anorak and pulled it off. Her sweater was damp but the rain hadn't actually soaked it, she decided.

'The sweater too,' Jamie Knox said tersely.

'It's okay!'

He took one long stride and caught her shoulder, his hand moving along the sweater. 'As I thought—it's damp, the rain soaked right through your anorak, didn't it? Get it off! You aren't sitting around in damp clothes all night.'

She pulled free, her dark blue eyes stormy. 'I'm not sitting around naked, either. I haven't got anything on underneath it.'

His mouth went crooked with impatient amusement. 'You crazy female! Don't you even know what to wear for a day on the fells?' He unzipped his own anorak, which had, she saw, a warm waterproof lining, stripped off his sweater and then pulled off the cotton shirt he wore under that. Melanie watched, backing, her eyes alarmed.

'What are you doing?'

He threw her the shirt. 'No need to get excited. I'm not about to make a pass. Take off your sweater and jeans and put this on. You're so small and skinny it should come to your knees.' He put his sweater on again and turned to attend to the fire, talking without looking at her. 'Hurry up. I'm not watching, and if you could see yourself you wouldn't be so scared I might make a pass at you. You're covered in mud, your hair's like wet string; you are a very bedraggled object, Miss Nesbitt. My male instincts aren't going to run amok at the sight of you, naked or otherwise.'

She hurriedly took off her sweater and jeans and slid into his shirt. It was still warm from his body and carried his scent; male, faintly musky. It clung to her and she smoothed it down, feeling odd about wearing his clothes.

'Now put my anorak on,' he said, 'Mine's more weatherproof than yours; the rain didn't penetrate it.' A shower of sparks flew up as he put another log on the fire, which was burning nicely now.

'Are you sure you'll be warm enough?' Melanie said hesitantly.

He gave her a dry smile. 'Quite sure.' He began rummaging in his rucksack and produced some thin twine. 'I'm going to stretch this across the chimney breast; it will make a nice drying-line for your clothes.'

'You think of everything, don't you?' she said with faint hostility.

'I try, Miss Nesbitt.' The black head turned, he grinned at her, wicked charm in his face. 'To tell you the truth, the nails are there—I'm not the first person to have the idea. I told you, this place is often used by climbers caught out by the weather.'

She looked in her own rucksack. 'I have some

hot coffee left,' she offered. She unscrewed the top, grimacing. 'Well, warm coffee, anyway.' She poured some and held it out to him and he came over to her and sat down beside her, taking the plastic cup, sipping the coffee.

'Thanks, this is very welcome. What else have you got in there?'

'Biscuits and an orange and a little slab of cheese.'

He smiled, his eyes crinkling. 'Then we shan't starve, shall we? I brought Kendal mintcake, a couple of apples and a flask of tea.' He finished the coffee and held out the cup. 'Now you have some—it will make you feel more human, believe me. I feel better already.'

She managed an answering smile and poured herself half a cup. Holding it between her palms to let the warmth percolate her skin, she glanced at him apologetically. 'I'm sorry to have got you into this. It isn't going to be very comfortable, is it?'

'Not exactly,' he agreed without resentment. He had very long black lashes, she noticed, and his skin was smooth and tanned over those sharp cheekbones. 'June told me that your fiancé was supposed to be coming, but backed out—did you have a row with him?'

'No, I did not,' she denied, scowling. 'Why should you think . . .'

'Pure guesswork! You were obviously angry when you arrived—and it wasn't just because I'd taken your parking space. You over-reacted about that. I could see you were in a mood to bite the first person who gave you an excuse. You were mad with the guy in your life—so with typical female logic, you decided to go off alone and take risks just to show him!' He got up and began to arrange her jeans and sweater on his taut washing-line above the fire.

'That's not true!' Melanie said angrily. There was, of course, enough truth in his speculation to make her furious with him. She and Ross hadn't had a quarrel, but only because Ross hadn't stayed long enough and she hadn't had a chance to lose her temper. Ross rarely gave her any opportunity to let him see how she felt, in fact. The pent-up frustration made her look at Jamie Knox with smouldering eyes. She might not be able to confront Ross, but Jamie Knox was just a few feet away and she could tell him just what she thought of him.

'Your guesswork is light-years off course, and pretty insulting, too. I made a stupid mistake, but I'm not a complete fool. If I was angry with my fiancé, I'd tell him, I wouldn't punish him by trying to kill myself. You know nothing about me so don't dream up fantasies to explain what I do.' Anger made her voice shake and he leaned on the chimney breast, listening with derision in his eyes.

'Did I hit a button?'

Her flush became red-hot. He had, of course, damn him. She tightened her lips, not daring to risk a reply to that.

After a pause during which she heard the rain beating against the dirty window and the crackle of the fire, Jamie Knox asked conversationally, 'What do you do for a living, by the way?'

'I work in an estate office,' she said curtly, staring at the smoke and flare of the fire.

'In Carlisle?'

She gave him a surprised look. 'Yes. You seem to be very well informed about me.'

'June told me,' he said, his mouth amused again, and she knew June well enough to understand why. June loved talking about her guests; she was a compulsive news-gatherer and passed on everything she learned to everyone else she talked to.

'What do you do and where do you live?' she asked pointedly, because why should he know so much about her when she knew almost nothing about him?

'I've got a cottage half a mile from the pub,' he said, and her eyes widened.

'You live here all the year round?'

He nodded, producing a slab of mintcake and breaking off a piece, which he offered her.

'Thank you.' She took it and nibbled it. 'And what's your job?'

'At the moment, I haven't got one.' He got up and threw another handful of pine-cones on the fire. Their aromatic scent reached her nostrils and she leaned forward to inhale it with pleasure as she answered him.

'Were you made redundant?' Her voice was sympathetic now; it had happened to several people she knew. Unemployment was very high in this part of the country, even more so in the big urban centres within a few hours' drive of the Lake District, of course. He had a very expensive car, presumably he had had a good job. He must have had a shock when he lost it.

'More or less.' His voice was dry. 'Don't look so sorry for me—I'll get another one. No need to pass round the hat just yet.'

She smiled at him, her dark blue eyes gentle. 'It must be very worrying, though. I'd hate the uncertainty.'

He considered her, his head to one side. 'Yes, I suppose you would. You look very highly strung—

it must be those fine bones of yours. You seem fragile, as though you snap under pressure.'

Her chin went up; his voice held what she thought to be a note of dismissal. 'I'm not fragile and I don't snap under pressure!'

'You're snapping now!' His mouth was crooked and she sat back, biting her lip.

'You're a very irritating man, Mr Knox.' Turning away, she looked in her rucksack for a comb and began to drag it through her damp, tangled hair, crossly aware that he was watching her.

'I wish I could wash my face,' she said, wondering how she looked, although what difference did it make? She wasn't trying to attract him, she didn't care what he thought.

'Why not? I'll fetch you some water, although it will be very cold.' He got to his feet and she stared at him in surprise.

'Water? Where from?'

'There's a rain barrel right outside the door. Don't you notice anything? You weren't in the Girl Guides, were you? When you're in strange terrain, it pays to keep your eyes open.'

'You try keeping your eyes open when someone's carrying you over his shoulder!'

'I'd like to see the guy who tried,' Jamie Knox said, laughing. 'Can I borrow my anorak for a second?' She took it off and he slid into it and headed for the door. As he opened it, a gust of wind blew in, bringing rain, and Melanie shivered, crouching closer to the fire. He was back a moment later, carrying a rather rusty old bucket.

Melanie washed hurriedly, conscious of his stare, and dried her face on a handkerchief.

'You'd better put my anorak on again,' he said softly. 'My shirt seems to be rather transparent in firelight.'

She glanced down hurriedly, her cheeks burning as she saw the way the thin material of his shirt clung to her body, outlining the dark circles of her nipples. He must be able to see every inch of her, as if she were naked. Melanie put out a hand blindly as he took off his anorak. She couldn't look at him. She fumbled her way hurriedly into the garment and zipped it up with shaky fingers.

Jamie washed his own face and dried it, while Melanie stared fixedly at the fire. They were alone here; she knew nothing about him. What if he suddenly grabbed her? She would have no chance of fighting him off. She eyed him secretly through lowered lashes. The black hair was plastered to his skull by rain, showing her the powerful contours of a face which disturbed her. She couldn't begin to guess what he was thinking.

'It's raining hard out there,' he said. 'By the way, there's a pretty primitive outhouse at the back, if you need it.'

Her flush deepened. 'Can I borrow your torch?'

'You'll need it,' he said, handing it to her as she got up. 'By the time you get back, your sweater should be quite dry. You'll feel more human when you can get dressed again.'

She avoided catching his eye, but she was relieved by the remark. Had he meant her to be relieved? Did he realise that she was alarmed by being alone with him here?

She limped round the hut, her head bent against the cold, driving rain, the faint circles of light from the torch showing her where she was going, the wind howling on the fells. She came back a few moments later, drenched and with chattering teeth. The outhouse had been even more primitive than her worst imaginings, and more than that, she had seen something with a tail in there.

'There are rats in it!' she said, bursting back into the hut and slamming the door after her, to drip her way back to the fire.

'Probably,' he said coolly, watching her take off his sodden anorak. Melanie pulled her sweater off the line and hastily put it on, her head averted. Her jeans were dry, too; once she was fully dressed her nerves stopped jumping every time he moved. As she sat down, huddling next to the fire, he produced a leather flask and handed it to her.

'What's this?' she asked.

'Brandy, just what we need to put some warmth back into us!'

She shook her head. 'Thanks, but I don't like brandy.'

'You don't have to like it. Swallow some, it will do you good. Your hair's soaked again; a pity neither of us thought of bringing a towel.'

'Isn't it?' she muttered sarcastically. 'Next time I get lost I'll remember to bring one.'

'That isn't so funny, Miss Nesbitt,' he said with dry amusement. 'I've only known you a short time, but I get the feeling you're prone to get lost.'

Melanie frowned, pointlessly rubbing her hand-kerchief over her hair in an attempt to dry it a little. She wasn't sure what he meant but she didn't like the way he had said it.

He moved, and she grew tense again. 'Stop arguing and drink some of this brandy,' he said, holding the flask to her mouth. 'You don't want to get pneumonia, do you?'

'You bully,' she said with animosity. He smelt of rain and woodsmoke, his face inches from her own. She glanced through her lashes at his brown cheek; the hooded dark eyes watched her from hiding, their gleam unnerving. A pulse of panic beat in her throat. To hide that, she reluctantly swallowed some brandy with a shudder. It went to her head; she felt almost dizzy.

'Feel better now?' Was he laughing at her or was that crooked little smile meant to help her relax?

She stared into the fire, watching the blue and orange tongues of flame curling round the wood. Jamie Knox drank a little brandy, sitting next to her, his knees bent up and his chin resting on them.

'What are you seeing in the fire?' he asked casually a moment later. 'Pictures? I remember doing that when I was small. At Christmas we used to roast chestnuts in the ashes; they tasted smoky and burnt, but that was part of the fun.'

'We did, too,' Melanie said, smiling. 'On a shovel—I liked hearing the chestnuts burst open. We made toast in front of the fire, too.'

'Instant nostalgia, a fireside, isn't it?' he murmured. He began to tell her about Christmases he had spent abroad, often in hot countries, and how much he had missed the traditions and even the cold wintry weather of home. He had travelled a great deal, presumably because his job took him all over the world. He talked casually but gave her vivid word pictures of places he had seen; Melanie was fascinated. Was he a journalist, she wondered?

'I haven't really travelled at all,' she admitted ruefully. 'Just a couple of holidays abroad—one year we went to Spain, and spent two whole weeks just lying on the beach. Last year we went to Italy and did some sightseeing in Rome and Naples. That was a coach tour, I found it rather exhausting. We only stopped in any place for two or three days. I got coach-sick.'

'We?' he queried, watching her intently.

'My family—we all went together.' She turned

her head and their eyes met; Melanie felt that odd quiver of panic again, although there was no real threat in his gaze. Hurriedly, she asked, 'Do you come from a big family?'

'No,' he said. 'Where's your fiancé this weekend?'

Her fine-boned, expressive face quivered with feeling at the abrupt question, and he stared at her, his eyes narrowed.

'Bahrain,' she said huskily. 'He travels a good deal, too.'

'Doing what? Business?'

'Yes,' she said.

'What sort of work does he do?'

'You ask a lot of questions,' Melanie said shortly, reluctant to talk about Ross.

'We must pass the time somehow,' he said, smiling mockingly. 'Of course, there are alternatives, but if you're in love with another man, I suppose you wouldn't be interested?'

Melanie turned her head towards the fire again, staring into the flames with fixed gaze but intensely aware of his every movement, every breath he took.

'Don't,' she said in a very low voice.

'Don't what?' He sounded amused still; she didn't find it at all funny.

'Flirt. This is difficult enough without you making it even harder.'

There was silence, then he laughed shortly. 'You're right, of course. I apologise. The trouble is, Miss Nesbitt, you're a very attractive girl and this is a very intimate situation we're in—I'd have to be superhuman not to . . . well, let's just say that your fiancé must be crazy. What's his name, by the way? As we're always talking about him, I might as well know who I'm talking about.'

'I don't want to talk about my private life at all,' she said. 'But his name is Ross.'

'Surname?'

'No, that's his first name. Ross Ellis, if you insist.'

There was another silence. She looked around, sensing something odd in the air, and saw his eyes narrowed, hard and black.

'Ellis? The Ellis who runs the big construction company?'

Slowly, she nodded, wondering what he was thinking. The humour had vanished from his face, no doubt because he had been impressed by hearing that she was engaged to one of the most important men in the north-west. Ross had inherited a construction firm which until that time had been a purely local company in this area. Ross had built it into a worldwide company in just fifteen years. He was a man of dynamic energies. Whenever she was upset because she never saw enough of him, she reminded herself that Ross was in the habit of giving his entire attention to his firm. He simply hadn't realised yet that she needed him, too. If he would only stay still long enough to listen to her, she might make him understand that. He must love her, or why would he ask her to marry him?

'I'd heard he had got engaged,' Jamie Knox said slowly.

That didn't surprise her. The announcement had caused quite a bit of local interest. Ross was a big local employer; naturally people took an interest in everything he did. Melanie had been rather nervous when she had to be interviewed by reporters, but Ross had been there too and he had smoothed over her hesitations and stammered answers.

'Do you want anything to eat? A biscuit? An orange?' Jamie asked and she shook her head.

'June packed a huge lunch for me—oh, they must be worried by now, wondering where we are!'

'I told them that if I found you, I'd bring you here. With binoculars they'll be able to see the light in the window and guess that we got here safely.'

She gave him a daunted look. 'You really do think of everything, don't you?' There was something very disturbing about that.

'If I can,' he said with an oddly wry smile. 'Sometimes things happen that you couldn't possibly foresee—but that apart, I try to anticipate what I may meet before I set out. If we haven't started down at first light, June and Fred will call the mountain rescue people, but they'll wait until then. Nothing could be done in the dark, anyway, not with this rain and wind. They couldn't even get a helicopter up here to take a look around.'

Melanie was beginning to feel very sleepy; the brandy, no doubt. She lay on her side, the straw was comfortable enough, she was warm and dry and very tired. Her lids grew heavier and heavier. Through them, half-closed, she secretly watched Jamie Knox gazing into the fire, as unblinking as a cat, his knees up, his chin on them, his rakish profile all that she could see of his face. She wondered about him. He was rather secretive for a man who asked so many questions. Her lids drooped. She couldn't keep them open any longer and she slid into sleep.

She woke when something touched her cheek. Her lids stirred, she drowsily opened her eyes and looked up straight into Jamie Knox's face. Still locked in half-sleep, Melanie stared at him as if she had never seen him before, bewildered by his presence in her dream, but then her heart began to beat faster and faster, she went cold and then hot, with shock and memory. In a flash she remembered where she was and who he was, and then she felt a stab of fear as he bent closer.

'Wake up, Sleeping Beauty,' he murmured, smiling, his mouth inches away.

She knew he was going to kiss her. For a second her muscles stiffened; then his lips touched her mouth, warm flesh, softly persuasive, and Melanie jack-knifed upwards, pushing him away.

He went without resistance and got to his feet. 'Obviously, it works with a vengeance,' he said, puzzling her. 'I wonder if the original Sleeping Beauty slapped her prince?' He moved away without waiting for her reply. 'Time to start down, Miss Nesbitt. It's almost light and the rain has stopped. It is going to be a beautiful morning.'

Melanie sat there for a moment, breathing hard. The hut was filling with pale grey light, and the fire was out. She shivered in the chill of the stone walls and the early morning, and felt strangely depressed.

CHAPTER THREE

'OF course, you mustn't drive a car until the swelling has quite gone down, it wouldn't be safe,' said the doctor as he finished binding her ankle, and Melanie forced a smile, nodding. She hadn't thought of that aspect of her accident. She would have to ring the family and ask one of them to drive over to pick her up, and that would mean telling them the whole story. She didn't look forward to doing that.

When the doctor had left, hurrying to get on with the rest of his round, June considered her unhappy face and patted her shoulder.

'Don't look so down, lovey. I tell you what, Fred was going into Carlisle some day this week to pick up some things I want from the Lanes. Wonderful new shopping centre, I wish it was nearer here. Whenever I go to Carlisle I head straight for it. Anyway, I'll get him to go today, he can drop you off at home and do my shopping at the same time, then you can pick up your car any time you like. We'll look after it for you; it will be safe in our car-park.'

'Thank you,' Melanie said gratefully, but when Fred came into the kitchen he had Jamie Knox with him and the two men had already hatched another scheme.

'Jamie's going to drive you home, Melanie,' Fred told her. 'And I'll drive over to Carlisle this afternoon, after the bar shuts, to do June's shopping

45

and pick Jamie up afterwards. You don't want to leave your car sitting around in our car-park for days, do you?'

Melanie said flatly that she didn't. 'Thank you, Fred. You're very thoughtful.'

'It was Jamie's idea,' Fred said generously, as if he needed to tell her that.

She turned a tight smile towards Jamie Knox. 'Thank you.' She didn't want him driving her home, she didn't want her family to see him, to ask questions, to be curious about what had happened between them. She knew that last night had been totally innocent, and of course her uncle and aunt would believe her when she told them that nothing had happened, but something about Jamie Knox's bright, amused eyes and cynical smile made her feel absurdly guilty, as if she were lying. Yet she didn't quite dare to refuse his offer because that might make Fred and June curious, and so far they hadn't raised any eyebrows or looked askance over the explanation of how Melanie and Jamie had spent the night in the shepherd's hut. Such things happened all the time in this district; people were always getting lost in the hills or trapped by bad weather. The important thing was that they had got safely back, that was all that June and Fred cared about, and no doubt Uncle Teddy and Aunt Dolly would feel the same, but Melanie would still rather not let the family meet Jamie Knox.

Meeting his gaze, she was certain he could read her mind and was amused by everything she wasn't saying.

June helped her pack and Fred carried her case down to her car. She got hugs from both of them and messages for the family, then Jamie Knox started the car and shot out of the car-park.

Melanie was aggrieved to see that he could get more speed out of her old car than she ever had.

'It might be faster by mule,' he observed as he followed the winding road beside the lake. Maddeningly, the weather today was gorgeous; the sky clear, the sun bright, the hills a sharp outline on the horizon.

'You're doing forty miles an hour. What more do you want?' she muttered, settling reluctantly into the passenger seat next to him. 'I don't believe in driving too fast, anyway, especially not on these roads.'

He looked sideways through his lashes at her. 'Did you ring your family and tell them what had happened?'

The heat in her face was answer enough and her silence underlined it.

'He whistled softly. 'Going to?'

'I'll tell them whatever suits me,' she said defiantly.

'You've got to explain that bandaged ankle somehow!'

'Anyone can have an accident walking the fells!'

'Do June and Fred know that our night on the bare mountain is a deadly secret?'

'Oh, be quiet!' she wailed, because of course she couldn't ask Fred and June to lie for her and sooner or later the whole story would come out.

'June tells me your parents are dead and you live with an aunt and uncle,' Jamie informed her, undeterred.

Furiously she snapped, 'Did they forget to mention my two cousins and the cat?'

'Cats didn't come into the conversation,' Jamie murmured. 'There was some talk of a Liz and a Will who both like to sail. How do your family get on with your fiancé?'

Melanie averted her face, staring out at the russet colours of oak and elm, the scarlet of rose hips and haw berries in the hedges. Autumn was in its early days, there were still lingering signs of summer here and there—a few last roses, rich green grass in pastures.

'Very well, thank you,' she said stiffly. What was he implying now? 'What job did you say you did? You aren't a policeman, by any chance? Or a tax inspector? You seem very fond of asking questions about things that have nothing to do with you.'

'I'm interested—any reason why I shouldn't be?'

She turned, her dark blue eyes very wide and startled. 'In what?'

He turned his head and their eyes met and her heart skipped a beat. 'In you,' he said softly, watching the betraying colour run up to her hairline.

Melanie hurriedly looked away again and kept her head turned as she answered huskily. 'I asked you not to do that . . .'

'Do what?' he teased, turning off to get on to the motorway.

'Flirt. You knew I meant that! It may be just a game to you, but I don't play that sort of game, Mr Knox. I'm engaged and I love my fiancé so please stop talking to me like that.'

They were beginning to put on more speed; it made her nervous to find herself in the fast lane, passing cars which would normally pass her, but Jamie Knox was coaxing a surprising power out of her old vehicle. She hoped he wasn't wrecking the engine for ever.

He seemed to have nothing to say in response to her and they drove in silence for a while, until he asked suddenly, 'How old were you when your parents died?'

'Thirteen,' she said, reluctantly, because she was beginning to feel that every scrap of information he wheedled out of her was a hostage to fortune and might be used against her at some future time. Talking to Jamie Knox was like being under X-ray—Melanie felt mentally naked, her innermost thoughts and feelings observed and speculated upon. She didn't like it, especially as she didn't quite trust the man. It was more than distrust now, though; she was half afraid of him.

'Thirteen? I see,' he drawled, and she made the mistake of looking round at him, her blue eyes apprehensive. It was dangerous to ask, she knew that, but she couldn't resist the nag of curiosity.

'What do you see?'

'Losing your father in your early teens must have had a traumatic effect,' he murmured coolly. 'And Ross Ellis no doubt makes a great father figure.'

She went rigid with anger. 'Don't try that cheap psychology jargon on me, Mr Knox—it won't work. We don't know enough about each other for you to have a clue what makes me tick. We're practically strangers.'

'Are we?' he asked drily, apparently untouched by the ice in her voice.

'We only met this weekend and . . .'

'Time is relative. How long have you known Ross Ellis?'

'Mind your own business.' Her throat was hot with resentment and helpless fury. 'Please don't keep needling me, Mr Knox. Just concentrate on your driving. I don't want to talk any more. You've given me a headache.'

He laughed. 'That tired old female excuse! I'm ashamed of you.' But he lapsed into silence as she asked and it wasn't long before they were on the

outskirts of Carlisle. Melanie broke their silence to
tell him how to get to her home. With any luck,
nobody would be in because at this time of day
Aunt Dolly was often out shopping. She had a set
routine; had coffee in the pedestrian precinct and
then enjoyed a walk round the Lanes, the new
shopping centre which brought so many people to
Carlisle from the surrounding area. Sometimes
Aunt Dolly met a friend for a snack lunch before
coming home.

Jamie pulled up outside the old, white-painted
gate and sat forward, his hands resting on the
wheel, to stare up at the ramshackle Victorian
house. It had been built in 1832, by a prosperous
Carlisle corn merchant with a large family and
several servants. There were seven bedrooms, a
huge and draughty drawing-room, a panelled dining-
room and a muddle of other rooms downstairs,
often oddly shaped and very eccentric in design. It
was hardly convenient or modern but it had a
certain style and character and the Nesbitts loved
it, even Aunt Dolly, who had to do most of the
housework, except at weekends when Liz and
Melanie helped her. As Aunt Dolly always said,
'You can tell the man who had this house built
expected someone else to keep it tidy. All very
well for him—all those servants! How much easier
life was in those days.'

'Except for the servants,' Liz usually said in her
dry way, and Aunt Dolly would laugh and say that
Liz was so down to earth, not at all romantic.

'A very handsome house,' Jamie Knox murmured,
his eyes flicking over it from the delicate fanlight
above the door to the little gables in the roof. The
shabby stucco had a creamy glow in the sunlight;
the house looked loved and contented, the small
garden in the front was rich with dahlias and

chrysanthemums; golden amber, rust, dark blood-red. A spiky cluster of Michaelmas daisies bloomed near the wall, their petals visited by bees and butterflies on this surprisingly summery morning, so that the air was full of a busy hum, a flutter of wings.

'Thank you for driving me back here,' Melanie said stiltedly. 'And for . . . for everything you did.' She felt ungrateful—he had, after all, gone to a lot of trouble for her and she hadn't really thanked him properly. She would have been more fervent in her thanks with almost any other man, but Jamie Knox had made it difficult for her to be too nice to him. He might misread friendliness. He seemed to misread most things.

He got out and came round to help her down, his hand under her elbow. 'I'll see you to the door then come back for your case,' he said, urging her towards the gate.

'I can manage. The case can stay in the car for the moment,' she said firmly, and glanced up the road. 'If you walk to the top of this road you'll get a bus straight into the centre of town. They're very frequent and it isn't far.'

He didn't relinquish her arm, indeed his fingers tightened on it.

'Got your door key?' he enquired, somehow managing to make her keep walking through the gate and up the path with its black and white Victorian tiles, laid in a symmetrical diamond pattern. A few had been cracked over the years, and some were missing altogether, but the path had a certain style, like the house, which Melanie loved.

He was still being kind; she didn't like to dismiss him too peremptorily, so she produced her key and he took it and inserted it into the door.

The door was reluctant to open; it needed oiling but none of them ever remembered until the matter became crucial, and the heavy rain over the weekend had obviously warped the timbers further, because when Jamie pushed it politely the door didn't budge and he had to let go of Melanie to use his full strength on it.

At his shove, the door fell open with a protesting creak and Jamie tumbled into the house leaving Melanie outside, which was why Liz, seeing a complete stranger crashing through the front door, leapt down the last two stairs and faced him with one of her father's walking sticks grabbed up from the hallstand.

'Who are you?' she asked firmly. 'And what are you doing?'

Melanie hobbled into the hall at that instant and her cousin's voice halted.

'Melly? What's wrong with your foot?' Trust Liz to be so sharp-eyed and observant, thought Melanie, hurriedly smiling at her.

'I had a tumble when I was climbing, it's nothing much, just a slight sprain.'

Liz slowly slid the walking-stick back into the hallstand, her eyes moving to Jamie Knox enquiringly.

'I drove her back because she couldn't drive with one ankle out of operation,' he said lightly, smiling. 'My name's Knox, Jamie Knox. You must be Liz—I've heard a lot about you.'

Liz's eyebrows arched. 'Really? All of it good, I hope.' She glanced at her cousin with interest. 'You *have* had a busy weekend.'

Melanie's cheeks stung with hot colour and she looked away. It was bad luck finding Liz at home.

'Why aren't you at work?' she asked, wishing Liz hadn't seen Jamie Knox—or that Jamie Knox hadn't met her cousin, she wasn't sure which was the more worrying.

'I've taken a day off,' Liz said. Melanie should have remembered the complicated rota system by which Liz worked four days one week, five the next; a shift system made even more complex by the addition of paid annual holidays which Liz could taken *en bloc* or piecemeal thoughout the year. 'I'm working on the economics article I'm supposed to have ready by Wednesday,' Liz added. 'I can work better at home—no interruptions.' She paused, grimaced. 'Usually,' she said, her eyes smiling as she glanced at Jamie Knox.

'Did we interrupt?' he chimed in immediately. 'Sorry about that, but it must be nearly lunchtime—weren't you going to eat?'

Liz looked amused. 'I suppose I was, sometime, I think my mother left me some cold roast lamb and a salad—she's having lunch with a friend in town. I expect there'll be enough for three.'

Aghast, Melanie said, 'Oh, Mr Knox isn't . . .'

'Thanks, I'd love to stay for lunch,' he overrode her.

She turned angry eyes up to him. 'You've got to meet Fred in Carlisle, don't forget.'

'Not until five o'clock—that was the time we arranged, to give Fred time to get here and do June's shopping.'

Liz listened with interest, watching them both, her cool face alert and attentive.

'You know Fred and June? How are they? I haven't seen them for weeks.'

'Oh, they're fine—wonderful, aren't they?' Jamie put his shoulder to the front door and forced it shut. 'These hinges need oiling, you know—have you got an oilcan? I'll do it for you now. It's a mistake to let these little problems drag on; you have to deal with them as soon as they come up.'

Liz looked amused. 'How very forceful. Yes, there must be an oilcan in Dad's toolshed. Come and get it. He never throws anything away, even if he has no intention of using it.'

They walked away along the hall and Melanie followed grimly. Her heart had sunk as she recognised that Jamie Knox had no intention of going. He had shamelessly angled for that invitation to lunch—what was so surprising was that Liz had offered it in response to his blatant hint. It wasn't like her; she was usually rather cool with strangers and particularly strange men.

Liz looked over her shoulder. 'You're limping badly. Why don't you use one of Dad's walking-sticks, Melanie?'

Jamie turned and recrossed the hall rapidly and came back with one of the sticks which he offered to Melanie with both hands, his smile mocking.

She was tempted to hit him over the head with it, but controlled herself. 'Thank you,' she said through her teeth, and perhaps her iciness was a mistake because she felt Liz watching her curiously. Liz scented a story; her news nose was twitching. The last thing Melanie wanted to do was arouse Liz's curiosity.

She had hoped to skate lightly over the explanation of what had happened last night, but it was obvious that she wasn't going to be able to do that with Jamie around, deliberately stirring up curiosity. Liz only had to take one look at him to guess that a night spent alone with Jamie Knox was unlikely to be incident-free.

'Were you staying at the pub, too?' asked Liz as they all went into the large, sunlit kitchen.

'No,' Jamie said. 'I live nearby—I've got a cottage beside the lake.'

Liz gave him an envious look. 'Oh, lucky you! I've always dreamt of having one. It must be heavenly, being able to look out across Ullswater every morning. Is your cottage old?'

'Eighteenth century, typical local architecture— very simple and solidly built of stone. When I bought it the previous owner assured me that Dorothy Wordsworth had once called in there to ask for a glass of water when she was on one of those long walks they used to take, but I expect he'd invented the story to help sell the place.'

Liz laughed. 'A lovely thought, though. I've always preferred her to good old brother William. He's a little too pompous for my taste.'

'Oh, you're one of those people who prefer to think Dorothy wrote the poems and William just borrowed her ideas?' Jamie was drily mocking and Liz made a face at him.

'I didn't say that.' They went out through the back door into the garden. 'The toolshed is over there,' Melanie heard Liz say.

Sitting down on one of the shabby old horsehair chairs, Melanie listened grimly to their fading voices. They were talking in a lively, friendly way as if they had know each other for years. Liz liked him. That was bad news. Jamie Knox was mischievous; who knew what he might say to Liz? Melanie wanted him gone, out of her life at once and for ever. He disturbed her peace of mind.

When they returned Jamie had an oilcan in one hand, a rag in the other. He went into the hall to deal with the front door while Liz laid the lunch on the table.

'Does your ankle hurt much?' she asked Melanie. 'You'd better take the rest of the week off work.'

'A sprained ankle won't stop me sitting behind my desk and doing what I always do,' Melanie said flatly.

Liz shrugged. 'Up to you.' She put the platter of cold lamb in the centre of the table. 'Where did you find *him*? He's quite something, isn't he?'

'Is he?' Melanie asked coldly.

Her cousin eyed her. 'You know he is! I couldn't quite make out how he happened to be the one who brought you back home. How did you meet him?'

'He was in the pub,' evaded Melanie.

'And drove all this way for a total stranger! How admirable.' Liz was given to sarcasm; Melanie ignored it. 'I suppose he does know you're engaged?' asked Liz.

'Of course!' Melanie said tersely.

'Of course,' Liz echoed with dry amusement. 'You wouldn't flirt with other men, would you? You're too devoted to Ross Ellis, although heaven only knows why you should be. You seem to see little enough of the man. Half the time he's abroad, and when he's back in the UK he never seems to have time for you.'

'Liz!' Melanie said harshly, going pale. 'Don't say things like that, it isn't true. Ross is just very busy, but if he didn't love me he wouldn't have asked me to marry him.'

Lis sighed, looking contrite. 'I'm sorry, Melly, I didn't mean to upset you, don't look like that—it's just that sometimes I get angry with you for being such a doormat. You let Ross walk all over you; you shouldn't, you know. Men don't respect you for it. If you stood up for yourself, Ross wouldn't be so casual with you.'

Melanie heard Jamie Knox's footsteps in the hall and hurriedly stumbled to her feet, her face drawn.

'I don't think I'll have any lunch. I'm not hungry.'
She hoped Jamie hadn't heard their argument. She
didn't want him to know any more about her than
he already did. 'I'll go up to my room and take a
rest,' she said as he came whistling into the kitchen.

'The door's moving freely again,' he told Liz
cheerfully, but at the same time shot Melanie a
probing stare sideways.

Thanks,' Liz said absently, watching her cousin
too. 'Melanie, do have a little lunch, the lamb's
very good.' Her smooth-skinned face held apology,
appeal. 'You can take a rest after the meal,' she
coaxed, touching Melanie's arm gently.

'No, really, I don't want anything to eat,' Melanie
said. She turned to go, then halted. 'Oh, thank
you, Mr Knox, for everything.'

'My pleasure,' he said drily.

She forced a smile. 'You're very kind. Well,
goodbye.'

'Oh, not goodbye,' he mocked. 'We're going to
see each other again.'

Her dark blue eyes held startled anxiety and he
smiled into them with maddening amusement.

'After all,' he added, 'you obviously visit
Ullswater frequently, and I'm there all the time.'

Melanie retreated, limping up the stairs into her
bedroom. She hated tension and that was what she
felt whenever she was near Jamie Knox. He seemed
to know the effect he had on her and enjoy causing
it.

She lay down on her bed and closed her eyes,
but she knew she wouldn't sleep. She had slept
well enough last night and, anyway, her mind was
working overtime, worrying about what Jamie Knox
was saying to Liz downstairs. How much had he
told Liz? He seemed to like her cousin and Liz
obviously liked him; she had said as much. Jamie

Knox was Liz's type, after all—sophisticated, sure of himself, experienced. He wasn't Melanie's type, though. She simply couldn't cope with him.

It must have been an hour later that she heard the front door bang and then the sound of a car driving off. Melanie swung off the bed and got to the window in time to see Liz's car vanishing round the corner. Liz must be driving Jamie Knox into the city to meet Fred.

Liz still hadn't got back by the time Aunt Dolly let herself into the house. Melanie was in the kitchen drinking some tea, watching the clock and wondering where Liz had got to and if she was still with Jamie.

'Hello, pet,' Aunt Dolly said, dumping her loaded shopping-bags on a chair with a sigh of relief. 'Had a good weekend? Very naughty of you to go off on your own like that. Liz could have gone with you. I was just going to suggest it when I heard you drive off.' She patted her silvery hair in front of the mirror over the mantelpiece. 'Was the weather fine?'

'Some of the time.' Melanie took a deep breath and said in a rush, 'But while I was climbing in the fells it turned misty and I had to spend the night in an old hut.'

Aunt Dolly swung, mouth wide. 'Melanie! All on your own?'

'No, there was someone else—June and Fred sent a friend of theirs up to look for me and guide me, so I had company.'

'A friend of theirs? Who was that? Anyone I know?' Aunt Dolly wasn't yet alarmed. She might have been if she had known in advance that Melanie was going to be stranded in a hut all night with a stranger, but as Melanie was here, safe, telling her about it, she wasn't as horrified as she might have been.

'I don't think so,' Melanie said vaguely. 'And I hurt my ankle—it's only a sprain, though, nothing serious, I'll be able to go to work tomorrow.'

Aunt Dolly exclaimed again. 'Have you seen a doctor?'

'Yes, he said it was a simple sprain. He bound it for me.'

'Let me see,' Aunt Dolly said, and gazed at the bandaged ankle, shaking her head. 'There! If you'd taken Liz you wouldn't have done that. It isn't sensible to go climbing on your own, you should have learnt that by now. How lucky that June and Fred knew where you were. I hope you thanked them for being so thoughtful. Where was this place where you took shelter? It couldn't have been very comfortable. Really, Melanie, you were silly, weren't you?'

It hadn't been quite as much of an ordeal as Melanie had feared, telling the family, and she was able to go through it again when Uncle Teddy came in with Will, but that time she had Aunt Dolly to help her out, adding a chorus of comment and explanation which took some of the tension out of Melanie herself. She could sit back and let Aunt Dolly tell the story, with a few frills and some embroidery. Aunt Dolly enjoyed telling people anecdotes; she had forgiven Melanie for running such a risk by now and almost seemed to have been there herself. She made it very dramatic—a daring mountain rescue. She had one detail wrong, of course. She had the impression that Jamie Knox was Fred's age, an old hand in the Lake District, a weather-beaten hill-climber old enough to be Melanie's father.

Melanie did not disillusion her. She didn't say

anything when Aunt Dolly looked at the clock and said, 'Liz must have gone out on newspaper business, after all. I suppose that tyrant of a news editor rang her up and bullied her into working tonight. Really, it's disgraceful the hours they want her to work.'

Melanie's dark blue eyes watched the regular movements of the clock hands. Liz had been gone now for three hours. What was she doing all this time, and was she doing it with Jamie Knox?

She went to bed early that night; Liz still hadn't put in an appearance. When Melanie got up for breakfast she found Will at the table eating egg and bacon as if he hadn't eaten for days. He gave her a grin, saying cheerfully that Liz had left a note on the kitchen table asking not to be woken up as she had got in late.

'I knew she had; she woke me up at some unearthly hour—two in the morning, I'd swear it was,' Will said, taking a slice of toast and spreading it with marmalade. 'She cleaned her teeth so noisily I had nightmares about it. Wonder what she got up to last night and who with? Who's the latest victim of her fatal charm? I don't know what guys see in her, I really don't. I've seen prettier heads on a pint of beer.'

'Don't be rude about your sister,' said Aunt Dolly, removing the toast from him firmly and putting it near Melanie. 'Now, Melly, you're to eat something this morning. I don't hold with you going off to work with nothing inside you.'

Melanie forced down a cup of coffee and a slice of toast before rushing off to work. She did most of the paperwork in the estate office. The firm handled several private estates as well as selling houses, offices and shops. The work was varied enough to keep her interested and the pay was quite good by local standards. There wasn't that much choice in the area and Melanie disliked the idea of working in a large office where she would specialise in typing letters or spend all day filing. In the smaller office she had more responsibility, did a wide range of jobs, and also met quite a few people every day.

Her boss was already in the office, checking an inventory. Looking up, he said at once, 'Melanie, you're limping.'

His son, Andrew, grinned. 'Old eagle-eye misses nothing. Did you fall or were you pushed, Mel?'

When she explained, George Ramsden shook his head at her. 'How many times have I warned you young people about fell-walking? It's dangerous to do it alone.' He had a strong Northumbrian accent and a face that looked as if it had been hacked out of local stone, but that belied his character. He was a very kind man.

'It won't stop me doing my work,' Melanie said, sitting down at her desk, and George Ramsden patted her shoulder with one raw-knuckled hand, smiling at her.

'Good lass. I'm off to the auction rooms. Old Hamish will have stuck the wrong labels on everything if I'm not there to stop him.'

When he had left, Andrew made some coffee and sat talking to Melanie until a customer came into the shop. She was the first in a long line; it was a very busy morning. Melanie hardly had time to think about anything but work, for which she was grateful. Just before she went to lunch, the phone rang. 'Oh, damn,' she said, but picked it up reluctantly. It was Ross.

'Where are you?' she asked huskily; he sounded very far away.

'Still in Bahrain. I've no idea when I'll get back.

Did you have a good weekend? I'm sorry I couldn't be with you, but you understand, don't you?'

'Yes, I suppose so,' she said uncertainly, and his voice came distantly.

'What? I can't hear you.'

'I only said I understand. This is a very bad line.'

'Melanie?' His voice was a whisper at the end of a tunnel. 'I can't hear you. There's no point in talking on a line like this. Can you hear me? I'm ringing off. See you when I get back.'

She replaced the phone slowly, remembering the first time she had ever heard his voice. He had rung to enquire about a building site in which he was interested. Melanie had been impressed by his deep, cool voice. For some reason it had made her nervous; she had stammered. It was a week or two before she actually met Ross in person and she had known the instant he walked into the office that it was the man she had talked to on the phone. His features matched the confidence of that voice. So often a face was disappointing after you had heard a nice voice on the phone, but not with Ross. He was even more than she had imagined.

He had asked her to have dinner with him that first day, and after that she had been caught up in a whirlwind. Ross was so busy; he had to snatch time for himself. Dinners, lunches, drives in the country—all hurriedly arranged, all too brief. When he asked her to marry him, she was feverish with disbelief and excitement, she hadn't even stopped to think, she had just said, 'Yes, oh, yes, Ross.'

Where had that feeling gone? It was all such a short time ago. She had been in love with him, hadn't she? She still was, wasn't she? But her head was full of question marks about the way Ross felt and, if she were honest, about the way she felt herself. And how would she ever find any answers if Ross was never here and had no time to talk to her? If he loved her, wouldn't he find the time? she thought, and then, again the questions surged into her head and found no answer.

She paused in the pedestrian precinct to look at a dress in a shop window, working out if she could afford to buy it. The colour was so pretty, a warm turquoise. She always looked good in blue.

'It'll suit you,' a voice said behind her, and she saw the wavering reflection of Jamie Knox in the shop window with a shock of surprise that made her pulses leap and flare.

'Oh, hallo,' she said reluctantly.

'Buy it,' he urged, but she shook her head and began to limp away. He kept in step. 'How's the foot?'

'Still painful.' She halted at the door of a small restaurant where she often ate. 'Well, I'm going to have some lunch, excuse me.'

'What a coincidence,' he said, and her heart sank. 'This is where I was heading, too.' He took her arm and steered her across the crowded room. There was only one table free and she couldn't think of a polite excuse for refusing to share it with him. As she sat down she looked at him through her lashes, suspicion in her blue eyes. Had he really been coming in here?

'Hallo, Jamie,' said the waitress, coming over with a broad grin. She never smiled at Melanie like that. 'We've got your favourite on, today— hotpot. Good, too. I had it myself.' She handed Melanie the menu with a nod of curiosity and Melanie ran a hurried eye down the list.

'I'll have soup and the chicken salad,' she said.

'Have the hotpot,' Jamie said, taking the menu from her. 'We'll both have soup and hotpot, Ethel.'

Melanie angrily opened her mouth to protest, but the waitress was already moving away and Jamie grinned mockingly at her.

'Their idea of a salad is two lettuce leaves and a wrinkled tomato. You'll be much better off with hotpot. My grandmother used to make it for me when I was small. She lived in Carlisle, we used to come and stay with her for Christmas, my mother, my sister and I, and she made us the best hotpot you've ever tasted. I don't know what she put into it, but I've never tasted one as good since.'

'She's dead?'

He looked at her with a wry smile, nodding. 'Years ago. She was eighty when she died; she'd had a good life, but I miss her. She was a wonderful old darling. One minute she was a tartar—if you'd done something she disapproved of! The next she was giving you a cuddle and everything was forgotten. She always said you should never let the sun go down on your anger, but she thought children needed discipline, especially when they had no father around to make sure they were kept in line.'

The waitress brought their soup, a Northumbrian broth made with barley. As they began to eat, Melanie asked, 'Your father was dead?'

He laughed, breaking off a piece of the crusty roll which had been brought with the soup. 'Not dead, no, but he was never there. He was in the merchant navy. Half the time he was on the other side of the world.'

Melanie's eyes widened. She watched him curiously. 'That must have been lonely for your mother, never having her husband there.'

Jamie looked up, shrugging. 'If it was, she never showed it to us. We had a wonderful childhood. When Dad was home it was always exciting, he brought us presents from all over the world and took us out, and then he'd go back to join his ship and things would be normal gain. Mum wrote to him several times a week, and read us bits from his letters, about where he was and what he'd seen. I had the best stamp collection in my class.'

'But he didn't get home for Christmas?'

'Rarely,' he agreed. 'That's why we always came to stay with Granny Carlisle. Mum thought we ought to have a family Christmas. Our other grandparents lived in London, my father's parents. Mum didn't get on too well with them. We didn't see much of them.'

Melanie finished her soup and watched his bent, dark head. It sounded a very interesting childhood. Did he take after his father? She wondered if he had gone to sea or had his father's long absences turned him against that idea?

Hesitantly, she asked, 'You said you hadn't got a job at the moment.' He might be sensitive about it; she wasn't sure how he would react to questioning.

He looked up, his face suddenly taut, the dark eyes hard. 'No,' he said through tight lips.

'You didn't go to sea, like your father?'

His face softened a little. 'I rather fancied the idea when I was small, but I got interested in other things and went to college instead. To my mother's great relief.' He grinned at her. 'She hadn't said a word, but I could tell she was heaving sighs of relief.'

Melanie laughed. 'She sounds great. Where does she live now?'

'She and Dad have retired. They live in Ullswater, just down the road from me.' His eyes held affectionate amusement. 'Keeping an eye on me and what I get up to even now!'

The hotpot arrived and Melanie had to admit that it was good; the lamb tender, falling apart as you touched it with your knife, the vegetables perfectly cooked and the flavour delicious. Jamie gave her a quizzical look, lifting one brow. 'Well?'

'You were right, it's marvellous,' she said.

'I'm always right,' he told her with maddening amusement.

Melanie gave him a look but didn't rise to the bait; she concentrated on the meal instead. When the waitress removed their plates and suggested a dessert, Melanie refused politely and just had coffee, and Jamie did the same. The hotpot had been far more filling than the lunch Melanie usually ate.

Jamie walked back with her to her office, talking about the fine autumn weather most of the way. She wanted to ask him if he and Liz had spent the evening together yesterday, but she was afraid that he would misinterpret her interest and imagine that she was jealous. He was conceited enough to jump to a conclusion like that. It wasn't true, of course. She didn't care who he went out with, but she was surprised at Liz.

'Why were you in Carlisle today?' she asked instead, and he made a wry face.

'I had to see my dentist—a half yearly check up. I hate dentists, don't you? Even when it is only a routine check I dread going.'

'You come all the way from Ullswater to see a dentist here?' she asked in disbelief, her face becoming suspicious. Did he expect her to believe that?

He considered her expression with dry mockery. 'He's been my dentist for years. I used to work here and he was the nearest good dentist. I've never got around to changing to someone else.'

She was about to ask him where he had worked, but as they reached the estate agency they walked straight into Andrew Ramsden who greeted Melanie urgently. 'Oh, great, you're back—I've got to go out to Penrith to see someone, can you hold the fort until I get back?'

'Of course,' Melanie said and Andrew handed her the keys to the office before rushing off. Melanie unlocked the doors again, gave Jamie a polite smile and said, 'Well, goodbye. I enjoyed the hotpot.'

She half expected him to linger, but he didn't, he nodded and walked away without a backward look. She watched him go with a strange feeling, biting her lip. She hoped she would never see him again, and at the same time that thought made her oddly depressed.

CHAPTER FOUR

THE following Friday was Will's birthday. He was twenty-three, although, as Uncle Teddy said, it was very hard to believe. Will still acted and moved like a teenager, either crashing about noisily or laughing like a hyena over nothing. Sometimes he didn't eat for hours without seeming to notice, but then he would come in at midnight and demolish every particle of food in the fridge or the larder. Bottles of milk vanished; cheese, cold meat, bread, fruit, all ready to eat and all gone next morning, so that his mother would survey her depleted resources and wail. 'Will's been at it again.' There was never any doubt as to the culprit; who else could eat so much at such an hour? Aunt Dolly knew without asking that Liz and Melanie were on a diet because they always were, and even if hunger came over them in the middle of the night they wouldn't eat everything that wasn't nailed down. Only Will would gorge like that.

But as today was his birthday his mother looked mournfully at her empty fridge and only said, 'I must go shopping.' She had cooked Will his favourite breakfast and he had departed for work with his father. 'Where's my list?' Aunt Dolly asked herself, looking about. 'I wish I hadn't said he could have this party, he's getting too old for birthday parties and his friends are so noisy. You will be here to keep an eye on them, won't you, girls?'

'Don't worry, you won't get back to find the police here investigating an orgy,' Liz said, laughing.

Flustered, Aunt Dolly said, 'Well, you never know—some of Will's friends seem very nice, but did you see that girl he brought round the other day—her hair was green and purple, and she had shiny orange marks on her face, like a Red Indian.'

'Tracy Simmons? She works at the Town Hall,' said Melanie, and Aunt Dolly looked incredulous.

'Well, whatever do they think there?'

'Not much,' Liz said drily.

Aunt Dolly began hunting for her shopping-list, muttering to herself. 'Where did I put it? I had it just now. Oh, look at that, how silly, I was holding it all the time, with my gloves. Melanie, come along, aren't I giving you a lift to work?'

Aunt Dolly and Uncle Teddy were going away for the weekend to the Lake District, so that they need not get involved with Will's party, and Melanie was secretly afraid that they might run into Jamie Knox. There was no hope that they wouldn't now hear June and Fred's version of how she came to be marooned for the night, but so long as they didn't meet Jamie that might not alarm them. One look at him, though, and Aunt Dolly would get agitated. The habit of worrying about Melanie was too ingrained with her.

Friday was always a busy day in Carlisle. People drove in from the surrounding countryside to shop, adding to the tourists who came to see the town, often staying overnight so that they could visit Hadrian's Wall. Of course, they were usually taken to Housesteads, the most spectacular of the forts on the wall, where they could park their coach beside the road in a walled car-park, have a cup of coffee and buy souvenirs and postcards before visiting the small museum. The more energetic

could then make the climb uphill to the fort itself,
to stand on the summit, buffeted by winds, staring
entranced at the incredible views on each side of
the wall, the misty green countryside falling away
in a sheer drop into echoing vistas.

While they were in Carlisle itself they had a
choice of either visiting the many shops or taking
in the cathedral. Melanie often had lunch there; it
was a short walk from her office and the salads
were beautifully prepared and inexpensive. Of
course, that meant that the Buttery was always
crowded with housewives, children, friends of the
cathedral, but the profits from the little restaurant
went to help maintain the cathedral structure. Built
of red stone—she always felt it had a baleful look
at sunset—it wasn't the most elegant of architecture.
Begun in the twelfth century, it was a strange
mixture of periods. Melanie preferred the original
style; there was something so beautiful about the
massive columns and Norman arches; their strength
had a confident simplicity. The cathedral was far
lovelier inside than out.

She was glad to be kept busy that Friday; it
stopped her thinking too much, wondering if Ross
was flying home, if he would soon ring her, if she
would see him today, tomorrow—soon.

Will's party didn't begin until eight and for
several hours before that they were all busy getting
the ground floor of the house ready for invasion,
clearing out most of the furniture, arranging chairs
and cushions on the floor, collecting tapes and
records, laying out the cold buffet in the kitchen.
Aunt Dolly had cooked most of it well in advance—
the spread was amazing, cold quiches, sausage
rolls, vol-au-vents, pizzas they would have to re-
heat, bowls of salad covered by cling-film, open
fruit tarts and gateaux. She had cooked the sort of

food she knew Will loved, but had done it in embarrassing abundance.

'She expects a plague of locusts,' Liz said, considering it all.

'Yum yum,' said Will, taking a sausage roll, and putting it into his mouth before his sister could stop him.

'Don't do that again,' Liz said, slapping his hand. 'Go and check that we've got enough glasses.'

'Done it. I've got my priorities right,' he said smugly.

The doorbell went and Liz groaned. 'Oh, no, they haven't started arriving already!'

Will looked at his watch. 'Nearly eight, not that early.' He danced off to open the front door while Melanie took off her apron and checked her appearance in the mirror over the fireplace. She had dressed for the occasion in what most of Will's friends would be wearing—smooth-fitting trousers and a casual top. Melanie's trousers were dark red velvet, her top cut quite low, sleeveless, glittering with black sequins. She had brushed her lids with a violet shadow that deepened the colour of her dark blue eyes, and her lipstick was a warm musk rose.

'I love that top,' Liz said, appearing in the mirror just behind her and assessing her own appearance coolly. 'You're lucky having such dramatic colouring; bold shades suit you.'

'You look pretty startling yourself,' Melanie teased her. Liz was normally very elegant but tonight she too had dressed not to look out of place among a crowd of Will's friends. Although the males at the party would be in their early twenties, they tended to bring much younger girls.

In her vivid poppy-splashed white shirt and tight green cords, Liz wasn't going to melt into the crowd.

Laughing, Liz said, 'I feel middle-aged faced with girls like Tracy Simmons. Do you realise, she's almost nine years younger than me? That's almost a generation. I look at her and ask myself— did I ever look that young?'

'No,' Melanie said, laughing back at her. 'You were horribly advanced for your age at eighteen. I was scared stiff of you.'

'You weren't?' Liz looked aghast.

'I was—you drawled everything you said and kept raising your eyebrows and smiling sardonically.'

'Oh, my Noel Coward phase,' Liz accepted resignedly. 'I must have been a horror.'

'I remember Aunt Dolly staring at your fingernails when you came in and waved them around—do you remember? You'd painted them black and your lipstick was a sort of mud colour. Poor Aunt Dolly, she was so horrified.'

'Not at all, it made life more exciting for her! She lived in a perpetual turmoil, never knowing what I'd be up to next. Think how much fun she must have had.'

Melanie laughed and behind them someone else laughed too, freezing the laughter on Melanie's face. She stared with stricken incredulity into the mirror, seeing Jamie Knox's face reflected there, dark, amused, unforgettable.

Liz turned, her smile welcoming. 'You're early— good. I'm so glad you could come.'

She had invited him? thought Melanie dazedly, watching them both in the mirror. They looked well together, she had thought so the morning Jamie drove her back here and he met Liz. They were talking as if they were old friends, casually at ease.

'Just as I drove up a vanload of kids arrived, too. Will is showing them where to park, but any minute now the balloon goes up. I hope you're prepared—boiling oil on the battlements and guard-dogs on the food? They looked a formidable collection to me.'

Liz laughed. 'Oh, I'm sure you can handle them—that's why I asked you. You're chucker-out-in-chief if things get rough, so look tough and sound dangerous.'

His black brows arched. 'Don't I always?'

'Now you come to mention it . . .' Liz said and at that minute Will yelled from the hall.

'Liz, where can they put their coats?'

'Well, here we go,' Liz said, vanishing.

The noise in the hall made it sound as if a riot had just broken out. Jamie pushed the door shut, his eyes on Melanie's back. She was still staring into the mirror fixedly, one hand restlessly tidying her immaculate black hair. She was afraid to turn round; that would mean admitting he was there, and Melanie wished he wasn't. Why had Liz invited him? Why wouldn't he get out of her life and stay out?

'How's the ankle?' It was a perfectly innocent question on the face of it, but it summoned up memories she preferred to forget and she felt her face burn.

'Much better, thank you,' she managed stiltedly.

He took a step towards her and she turned in agitation, stupidly afraid of having him too near her. She couldn't understand why she felt this instinctive alarm every time she saw him. He constituted a threat of a kind she had never felt before with anyone. Was she imagining the silent challenge he sent out? Perhaps her imagination was working overtime; her mind becoming feverish? Liz didn't seem to find him any problem. Perhaps it's just me? Melanie thought. I could be dreaming up conflicts which don't exist except in my own head.

'Ellis back yet?' He managed to make that question stiletto-sharp.

'Any time,' she muttered, angrily on the defensive.

'But he isn't going to come tonight? To the party, I mean?'

'I don't think he'll be back in time for that.' She was nervously twisting a lock of hair around her finger; it gave her something to do with her shaky hands.

'You don't seem to see much of him,' Jamie said, his mouth wry.

'Ross is a very busy man.'

'You're very understanding.' The sarcasm made her flinch and Jamie watched her nervous, restless fingers. His hand shot out and suddenly trapped them, pulling them down from her hair. 'Stop doing that. You're making me as edgy as you are.'

'I'm not edgy!' she lied, panic-stricken by his touch. His hand was cool and strong, and he was standing far too close.

'Aren't you?' His tone was almost angry now. He laid the fingertips of his free hand on her throat. 'No?' Under his touch she felt the savage beating of a pulse and was shocked by it. What was happening to her?

This was how he had been that night in the mist and rain; this was how she had felt every time he turned that dark stare towards her. It wasn't just her imagination, she wasn't losing her mind—Jamie Knox threatened her, his physical presence was overwhelming her at this instant, his touch was more than she could bear.

'Let go of me,' she said hoarsely, jerking backwards, and without a word he released her and turned away, pushing his hands into the back pockets of his black cord pants.

Melanie shot out of the room, but she took with her an indelible picture of his lean, prowling figure in the black pants and black sweater. Without a syllable he managed to set up echoes in her head. She fought her way through the cheerful throng in the sitting-room and began to help Will pour drinks for everyone, she smiled and answered when someone spoke to her, but she was in that other room, with Jamie Knox, vibrating with the anger coming out of him and confused by her own feelings about him.

She saw him with Liz some time later, circulating hot slices of pizza and trays of sausage rolls. Melanie stayed firmly behind the makeshift bar they had set up. She didn't drink anything but orange juice herself; she wanted to keep her head clear.

Liz drifted over with her tray and offered it to her. 'Better eat something while there's something to eat. You're going to need the blood sugar. Thank heavens this house is detached. If we had neighbours they'd be calling the police by now.' She had to use her voice on full volume to be heard above the music. Some of the guests were dancing now, others just sitting on the floor and talking, while some were wandering from group to group so that Melanie had long ago lost count of how many people were actually here.

Will had put the lights on dim; the room was shadowy and very stuffy.

'They've used up all the oxygen,' Liz said when Melanie mentioned that. 'At least there hasn't been any trouble.'

She spoke too soon. Half an hour later Melanie went to the front door when the bell rang and was almost knocked over by a crowd of gatecrashers who surged past her before she could check their identities.

Will was on his way out of the kitchen and said sharply, 'Hey, who are you? You weren't invited.'

Melanie reeled back against the stairs and took cover there as a fight broke out between the newcomers and Will's friends. As soon as Jamie realised what was happening he charged into the scrum and began hurling gatecrashers out of the front door by the scruff of their necks. Will and his friends followed suit. For a few minutes the hall was a heaving mass of struggling bodies, then the front door slammed and Jamie leaned on it, breathing thickly. Laughing like idiots, Will and the other boys went back to the party.

Melanie stole back downstairs, looking at Jamie's flushed face anxiously. 'Your cheek is bleeding. You'd better let me put a plaster on it.'

He straightened, a hand touching his cheekbone where a bruise was beginning to show. 'That certainly livened things up, didn't it?' He seemed unconcerned about the cut just below his cheekbone, but he followed Melanie into the kitchen and leaned against the draining-board while she got some boiled water from the kettle and some cotton-wool and gently began to clean the cut.

'Tell me if it hurts,' she said absently, her eyes fixed on his cheek.

'It hurts,' he said oddly, and her eyes lifted to meet his. 'That's better, you're always so reluctant to look at me.'

'Don't start that again!' Melanie muttered, concentrating on the cut, which was still bleeding. It was quite deep; perhaps he ought to have some stitches in it. It looked as if someone's ring had caught him—a heavy signet ring, perhaps?

'I make you nervous, don't I?' he said, as though that idea pleased him. 'You get very agitated when I'm around, that's why you won't look at me— while I'm looking at you, that is! I felt you watching me while Liz and I were handing round food a while back, but the minute I looked at you, you started staring somewhere else.'

She pretended not to have heard that. 'I think I ought to put some disinfectant on that cut, and it really should be seen professionally, it's very deep. You could go along to the casualty department at the hospital and see if it needs some stitches.'

'No,' he said coolly. 'It will be okay.'

'I'll get some disinfectant, then,' Melanie said, but before she took her hand away his hand covered it, held it there, against his cheek. At the same time his other hand went round her waist, pulling her closer.

Melanie had no chance to push him away before Liz came hurtling into the room. 'That fight has given them a new appetite—they want more food and . . .' Her voice stopped short as she saw them.

Melanie broke free and rushed past her, scarlet to her hairline. She couldn't face going back into the party. She ran upstairs to her bedroom. What must Liz have thought? Why did she have to come into the kitchen just then? Another minute and Melanie would have pulled away from him and there would have been nothing to see.

She closed the door, but didn't put the light on—she couldn't face the light, for the moment. Standing in the quiet darkness, she covered her face with her hands. Her skin was so hot. A strange mixture of emotions burned inside her. Why didn't he leave her alone?

She hadn't encouraged him. She had made it plain that she didn't want him to touch her. Was he like this with every girl he met? Was this how he was with Liz?

She forced her palms into her aching eyes—her head was throbbing with a sick headache. What sort of man was he, anyway? He ignored the fact that she was engaged to someone else—didn't he think it mattered? The anger grew inside her; all the words she never managed to get out when he was there were bubbling inside her head now. She despised him and he must despise her, of course, or he wouldn't ignore her protests and keep flirting with her.

Or did he think that secretly she wanted him to touch her? Her hands fell from her stricken face and she stared at the lamplit window of the room, all the colour and heat leaving her cheeks. Was that what he thought?

And on the heels of that came another, even more painful idea—was he right? She didn't even want to consider it, but once it had crept into her mind she couldn't push it out again. Did she secretly want Jamie Knox to kiss her? Hadn't she been on edge ever since she first saw him? She knew she had been very aware of him tonight from the minute he arrived; she had watched him whenever he wasn't looking her way, she couldn't deny it. When he was in the same room all her senses seemed involved with him; her ears picked up every nuance of his voice, her eyes kept finding him even when she tried not to look in that direction, her body temperature changed dramatically if he came too close, her skin intensely sensitive to his lightest touch.

She swallowed, frowning. She barely knew the man, why did he have this effect on her? What she did know about him she didn't like—of course she wasn't attracted to him! It was a crazy idea. He

made her nervous, that was all. He wouldn't take
no for an answer and she was kept on tenterhooks
worrying about what he might do next. Jamie Knox
was an infuriating man.

There was a tap on her door. Tense as a coiled
spring, she turned to stare as the door opened.

'Melanie?' It was only Liz, she realised, slackening
in relief. Her cousin peered across the dark room
at her. 'What are you doing up here in the dark?
Are you okay? Have you got a headache?'

'No, I'm fine,' Melanie said and Liz came right
into the room.

'I came up to warn you that some of those
gatecrashers are still hanging about outside. We've
rung the police and they're sending a car round, so
there's no need to worry, but we may have some
more trouble before the police get here. If you
hear a lot of noise, ignore it.'

'What are they doing?' Melanie asked anxiously.

'Nothing, at the moment—it's what they might
do that worries us.' Liz grinned reassuringly. 'I
thought I'd better warn you, in case it gets rough
out there. The police are on their way, so no cause
to panic.' She turned to go and Melanie said
huskily, 'Liz, wait!'

Her cousin came back. 'Yes?'

'Just now, in the kitchen . . . it didn't mean
anything. Don't take it the wrong way.'

Liz gave her a long, wry stare. 'I'm not taking it
any way at all. It's no business of mine if you
fancy Jamie Knox.'

'Of course I don't!' Melanie said shakily, her
face hot. 'I'm engaged to Ross, Liz, I wouldn't
play around with other men!'

'Ross Ellis is engaged to you, too, but I doubt if
he's as scrupulous as you are,' Liz said with sudden
irritation.

Melanie was taken aback. 'Ross wouldn't . . .' she began and Liz interrupted.

'Wouldn't he?'

'You don't know him,' Melanie said, staring at her cousin in bewilderment. Suddenly everyone was behaving oddly, she didn't understand what was happening. Liz had never cared for Ross much, but Melanie hadn't expected her to talk about him with dry ice in her voice, or to hint that Ross wasn't faithful to her.

'It's you who don't know him,' Liz snapped.

'What are you talking about? Ross doesn't make passes . . .'

'He made one at me!'

Melanie turned to stone on the spot. The light from the open door showed her Liz's face, an angry flush on it. Liz bit down on her lower lip as she stared back, then ran her hands through her hair violently as if wanting to tear it out by the roots. 'Oh, hell!'

Melanie stared at her, trying to speak; she couldn't. Her lips seemed numb, as if she had just had novocaine; her tongue hung heavily in her mouth. Liz groaned, staring at her.

'Melly, I'm sorry, it slipped out. I lost my temper. I didn't mean to tell you, I never meant to breathe a word about it, but I got so angry hearing you talk as if he was . . . you don't have to feel guilty if you did fancy Jamie Knox, don't be so blind. That's half your trouble: you're blind about people, you shouldn't be let out on your own.'

Melanie found her voice—or a voice, anyway, because she didn't recognise it as her own. It was very high and shaky.

'Ross made a pass at you? When?'

Liz looked uneasy, confused. 'Look, I'm drunk,

I think, forget it, Melly. As you just said, it didn't
mean anything—just another party . . .'

'What happened?' Melanie stared insistently at
her. 'Tell me the rest, Liz, you can't just leave it
now.'

'I wish to God I hadn't lost my temper,' Liz
muttered. 'I could bite my tongue out. Melly, don't
look at me like that—I didn't want to hurt you,
that was the last thing I wanted to do—why do you
think I never told you before? It was months ago,
anyway. It only happened once and as I said, it
was a party, and maybe Ross was drunk. I know I
was pretty euphoric, high as a kite until . . . well,
anyway, nothing much happened, a kiss, that's all.
Don't make a big deal of it, he never tried again.'

'What party?' Melanie asked flatly.

Liz sighed. 'That one his secretary gave when
she moved into her new flat, remember? What's
her name?'

'Brenda.'

'Yes, Brenda. She showed us her tiny roof
garden, you came out there too, remember that?
Then the rest of you went back in to dance and I
stayed out there—there was a moon, the most
amazing colour, almost orange.' Liz broke off,
swallowing, her face averted. 'Ross came back to
ask if I wanted a drink and I said look at that
moon, did you ever see anything like it?' Liz
shrugged. 'And then he kissed me.' She looked
almost wildly at Melanie. 'Look, I didn't invite it,
don't think I did a thing to make him think I
wanted him to—you could have knocked me down
with a feather. It was the last thing I expected and
I told him never to try that again. I pushed him
away and went back inside and I've hardly said
three words to him since. That was all there was to
it, and maybe parties bring out the beast in men!'

She tried to smile at Melanie, but her heart wasn't in it, and her smile withered as it was born.

Melanie turned her eyes away and stared over her cousin's head at the blurred orange glow of the street-lamp outside the window. She could hear voices outside. Were the gatecrashers regrouping for a new assault? It didn't seem to matter, she no longer cared about anything.

'Liz, go downstairs,' she said vaguely.

'Melly, don't take it so hard, for God's sake. I can't bear to see you look like that! It probably didn't mean a thing. A moment's aberration; men do have them—an impulse at a party when he'd had a few drinks. It's all my fault for telling you. I honestly didn't mean to, although I suppose you won't believe that now. It was months ago, Melly, after all, and he didn't do it again.' She stopped talking and watched Melanie's averted face. 'Are you listening?'

'I don't want to,' Melanie said, her jaws tight. 'I need to be alone, to think.'

'I can't leave you like this, Melly!'

'It's okay, I'm not breaking up.' Melanie tried to laugh but it came out so hoarsely that Liz groaned.

'Oh, hell. You look as if you are, you make me feel so guilty.' She took another deep breath and broke out with anger in her voice: 'You hear that? *I* feel guilty! Why should I be the one to feel like that? I didn't do anything. I didn't want him to, but then how do you ever know what's going on inside yourself? Maybe I was sending out vibes, maybe he thought . . .'

Melanie's eyes widened in surprise and sudden irony. So Liz felt that, too? Wasn't that what she had been saying to herself about Jamie Knox a few minutes ago? She had begun to wonder if she was secretly inviting, provoking him, if it was as much her own fault. Did women always feel guilty? Was guilt an instinctive female reaction in these situations—however innocent you thought you were, at first, did every woman sooner or later start to feel the nag of guilt?

Will called from the hall. 'Liz!'

They both jumped and before either of them moved Will's voice came again, from the stairs. 'Liz, Melanie—are you up there?'

'I'd better go,' Liz said. 'You stay here, then. I'll be back later.'

She hurried out, closing the door behind her, and Melanie sat on the edge of the bed feeling cold and tired. This had been quite an evening for shocks; they had come one after the other and she felt as if she were on a crazy switchback ride. The whole world looked strange to her; it was spinning and dipping around her. She felt she had to get up, stand on her feet, make everything seem normal again, grab at the familiar.

She walked carefully to the window to look out at the street. She had forgotten the gatecrashers. When she stared down, she saw them, by the gate, a dark cluster of thicker shadows just out of the circle of lamplight. Melanie saw them—and they saw Melanie. One of them had something in his hand. He raised his arm and threw; before she could duck out of the way something hit the glass with a violent crash.

CHAPTER FIVE

MELANIE screamed, covering her face with her hands in self-defence as jagged splinters of glass sprayed in all directions. There was a deafening confusion of sounds outside; people shouting, doors and windows opening as the people in other houses looked out to investigate the noise, the high-pitched siren of a police car coming nearer with a screech of tyres and the race of an engine, the thud of running feet as the gatecrashers dispersed, the slam of car doors as policemen jumped out when their vehicle braked to a halt followed at once by the noise of their heavy pounding pursuit.

When someone's arms went round her Melanie jumped about six feet in the air in shock.

'Are you hurt?' Jamie's voice was deep and rough; anger in it as well as concern. 'Melanie, let me see your face—did any glass hit you?' Still holding her with one arm he forced her hands down, turning her white face upwards. He had turned the light on in the room as he entered. She blinked, lashes quivering, in the vicious light, as he studied her. Melanie felt like a mole caught in a searchlight, and would have hidden her face again if Jamie's fingers hadn't ruthlessly controlled it.

'I don't see any blood,' he said to himself as his dark eyes flicked over her.

'I don't think any glass hit me,' Melanie said, feeling like hiding her face against him but refusing to give in to any such impulse. He might look comfortingly solid and protective, but she knew what any weak clinging would lead to, so she lifted her chin and tried to move away.

'Oh, yes, it did! Your hair's full of it.' Jamie's mouth was tight and harsh as he began picking fragments out of her hair, dropping them on her dressing-table where they glittered dangerously in the light.

Melanie didn't want to look at his hard-boned features so she stared at the broken window behind him. The night air came in; scented with chrysanthemums and rain. She heard the sudden swish of it on the pavements. This was city rain, washing the dust from the streets and gurgling in the gutters, but it still reminded her of the night they had spent together on the mist-shrouded hillside.

To dispel that memory, she said, 'Aunt Dolly is going to go crazy. Her worst nightmares come true! This is the last party Will is going to have for a long time.'

'It was hardly Will's fault. He didn't even know any of those little thugs by sight, nor did any of the boys. I made a point of asking them. No doubt the gang outside was prowling around and spotted a party going on and decided to muscle in for some free drink.' He brushed a palm over her crown slowly. 'I think I found it all, but you'd better wash your hair before you go to bed, in case I missed some.'

He had released her and she quickly stepped back, relieved to get away from him. 'Thank you,' she said stiffly.

'I expect the police will want to talk to you about what happened.'

Startled, she frowned. 'What can I tell them?'

'You were in here—you saw them, did you? You saw who threw the stone?'

He hadn't needed to ask what had done the damage because it lay on the carpet among the glass. She looked down at it.

'It's from Uncle Teddy's rockery,' she said flatly. 'I hope they didn't trample all his favourite plants.' She looked up at Jamie, her mouth rueful. 'I didn't actually see anything—I couldn't identify anyone, I mean. They were just dark shapes. They threw the stone deliberately, though.'

'At you?' he asked as if he knew the answer, as if it made him very angry.

She sighed, nodding. 'I suppose so. I looked down at them—maybe they thought I was laughing at them or something.'

'And maybe they're just mindless hooligans,' Jamie said thickly, his cheeks dark red with anger. 'They could have killed you. Or maimed or blinded you. Don't you realise how lucky you were? When I heard the crash and heard you scream I went cold. All the way upstairs I was wondering just what I'd see when I got in here.'

Liz came running up the stairs and burst into the room, her gaze hunting out her cousin and staring. 'Melly, are you okay? I was in the kitchen, I didn't hear anything until Will came in and said your window had been broken.'

'I'm fine. Have the police caught anyone?'

Liz shook her head. 'What a mess,' she said, looking at the glass littering the floor. 'That will have to be boarded up until we can get a glazier tomorrow.'

'I'll see to that,' Jamie told them. 'You go downstairs and wait in case the police want to interview you, Melanie. Liz, get her a stiff brandy and a cup of sweet tea.'

'I don't want . . .' she began.

'Don't argue!' Jamie instructed tersely.

Liz laughed. 'Come on, Melly, the man's in a temper, can't you see that? Never argue with a man in a temper. It's like crossing a field with an angry bull in it.'

Melanie went, talking to herself. 'I don't see why he should hand out orders as if he were God, or something. I don't have to jump when he says jump. Who does he think he is?'

'Talking to yourself is the first sign,' Liz told her.

'Of what?'

'Madness or love or both,' Liz said with her customary dryness.

'Yes, they're much the same thing, aren't they?' Melanie said fiercely. 'Anyone who falls in love ought to be put in a strait-jacket for their own protection until they fall out of it.'

It wasn't until she caught the stricken look Liz gave her that it dawned on Melanie how her cousin had taken that remark. Liz thought she was talking about Ross, about what Liz had told her!

Melanie paused on the stairs, touching Liz on the arm. 'That wasn't aimed at you! I didn't mean anything, I was talking wildly. It was all such a shock, this has been an eventful evening.' She laughed unsteadily. 'See how calm I am? I can even make understatements, not my usual style. Oh, Liz, for the moment let's just forget what you told me about Ross. Please?' She needed time to think, weigh up what she had learnt, and then she must talk to Ross himself before she really decided what to do, but she didn't want Liz going around looking like a wet weekend because she thought she had hurt Melanie. It would make life much easier if Liz was able to be natural again.

Her cousin looked sideways at her, oddly, frowning. 'Okay,' she said in a low, flat voice.

Melanie was deeply fond of her cousin. She knew that Liz was fond of her, too. They had never competed for their men, there had never been any jealousy between them. Liz might squabble with Will and Will might resent his sister's seniority and call her bossy and superior, with a tongue like viper, but Liz always went out of her way to be kind to Melanie. It was part of that family habit, perhaps. But it was also a genuine personal affection, and Melanie was quite certain that Liz hadn't wanted to hurt her, hadn't planned, deliberately, to tell her what Ross had done. Some women might do that—but not Liz. Some women might have set out to flirt with Ross—but not Liz. Melanie wasn't angry with her cousin, nor did she blame her for what had happened. She was stunned and in a bleak mood, but she had already absolved Liz from all blame.

The police arrived a few moments later. There wasn't much that Melanie could tell them, nor were any of the other guests much help. When the police left the party broke up. People seemed eager to get away, their party spirit had been dampened. Nobody had been hurt, but the window incident had been a shock to them—their gaiety had been shattered with the glass.

Liz and Melanie shut the door on the last one and turned back into the house just as Will and Jamie came from the garden with a sheet of plywood which they had tracked down in Uncle Teddy's toolshed.

'Make some coffee,' pleaded Will as he followed Jamie up the stairs, gripping his end of the wood. 'It won't take us long to board up your window, Melanie. I'm afraid the carpet is a bit wet—the wind's blown rain all over the floor, but it will dry out when the central heating gets to work on it.'

'I could do with some coffee before we tackle the tidying up,' said Liz, yawning.

'While you make the coffee, I'll start the washing up,' offered Melanie. Upstairs they heard banging. The men were fixing the board into the window.

'Mum will never get over this,' Liz said, setting out four mugs. 'Let's hope we'll be able to persuade a glazier to work on a Saturday. They're almost as hard to get as plumbers. If things look normal on Sunday night, Mum won't be nearly as frantic as she would be if she saw the mess the house is in now.'

'I expect Jamie will find a glazier,' Melanie said vaguely and then felt herself flushing, caught the quick glance Liz gave her. Hectically, she stammered, 'Well, he's that sort of man, isn't he? He always gets his own way, he makes things work for him.' That was what worried her about him—Mr Omniscient, All-Powerful Knox. Half the time she found herself doing what he told her to do, even if she started out by being determined not to fall into line.

She concentrated on filling the dishwasher with every item of china she could pack into it. Liz went off with a tray and came back with a few dozen glasses on it, then the coffee was ready and a moment later Will came down looking tired and gloomy.

'I'll never live this down. A fine birthday party this was! And now we've got all the clearing up to do!'

'Come and drink your coffee,' said Liz.

'Take it up to bed with you, Will,' Melanie urged. 'We'll tidy up before we come upstairs—no need for you to help. It can be a special birthday present for you. How's that?' She smiled at him coaxingly and Will looked uncertain, picking up his mug of coffee.

'I can't leave you two to do all the work . . .'

'I'll give them a hand,' Jamie said from the door. 'Off you go, Will. We'll manage very well without you.'

'I just bet you will!' Relaxing, Will grinned at him. 'Thanks for all your help tonight. You're not going to try to drive back to Ullswater at this hour, are you? Why not stay here? We can find you a bed, can't we, Liz?'

She turned from piling dirty plates on the draining-board, her brows shooting up. 'I'm not sure I like the way you phrased that!'

Jamie laughed and she grinned at him.

'If you don't mind sleeping in an attic . . .'

'Just love it,' Jamie said. 'I can sleep on a clothes line if I'm tired—an attic will be luxury,'

Will ambled to the door, his skin very white against the flame of his hair. He flapped a hand towards them. 'Night, everybody.'

'Goodnight, Will,' they said, watching his departure with sympathy. Poor Will. He couldn't be looking forward to what his parents had to say when they got home.

'I'll start washing glasses,' Melanie said, filling the sink with warm water. Liz went off with her tray to find some more and Jamie found another tray and followed her. Melanie stood at the sink, methodically washing the glass, her eyes abstracted as she thought about Ross.

In a sense, what Liz had told her was irrelevant to the real trouble between Melanie and Ross. She couldn't even guess why Ross had suddenly made a pass at Liz—from the beginning, the two of them had been distantly antagonistic, and Liz might be right when she said that it had been an impulse, that Ross had been drinking at a party and finding himself out there under the stars with an attractive woman had kissed her without thinking. It probably meant no more than that. It didn't mean that Ross was promiscuous, made passes at every woman he met. That simply wasn't in character.

And that was the core of the problem—Ross's character. Because once she'd thought that, she had come up against the question—what was his character? What did she really know about him?

When he came into the estate agency that first time, he had chatted her up, whisked her off to have lunch. It hadn't been what Liz would no doubt call a pass—Ross hadn't touched her with so much as a finger. He had watched her, smiled at her, asked her about herself, and she had never felt sexually threatened or thought that he was flirting with her.

Her busy hands stilled in the water; she stared at nothing, her face fixed and pale. When had he ever made her feel that he was deeply attracted to her? She couldn't remember a flare of real passion between them. He had proposed so soon after they met, though. She had been dumbstruck, staring back at him incredulously. He was asking her to marry him! And he meant it! Ross had smiled, taking her hands. 'Will you, Melanie? I want you to be my wife.'

The moment was sharp and clear in her mind. She closed her eyes, face bewildered. She didn't understand. If Ross didn't love her, why had he asked her to marry him? And if he did love her, why was there this distance between them? Why wouldn't he let her come any closer? She knew little more about him now than she had that first time they met, and whenever she tried to reach him Ross seemed to her to slam a door in her face.

There was a jangle of glass behind her. Jamie had come back with a loaded tray which he set down on the kitchen table. Melanie hurriedly got back to her washing up without looking round at him.

'Where's your vacuum cleaner?' he asked. 'I've picked up the glasses and plates in that room, but the carpet is going to need some work—it's littered with ash and peanuts.'

Melanie dried her hands and turned reluctantly. 'I'll do it.'

'I know how to use a vacuum cleaner,' Jamie told her with impatience. 'Where is it?'

She went over to the cupboard in which Aunt Dolly kept it but as she got it out, Jamie reached for it, his fingers touching hers, and Melanie jumped as if she had had an electric shock.

Jamie's voice was rough with anger. 'Don't do that! I'm a little tired of having you behave as though I was some sort of threat to you!'

She stared downwards, her neck bent, the black hair smoothly flowing against her cheek and shoulder and her lids hiding her eyes from him. He *was* some sort of threat to her, but she didn't want to admit it, even to herself.

'I realise you're upset, but don't take it out on me,' he said fiercely, when she didn't answer.

Melanie looked up, then, startled, her blue eyes wide and troubled. 'What are you talking about? Upset?' Her stare searched his hard-boned face and then she gave a little sigh. 'Oh, the stone through my window, you mean? Yes, it was . . .'

'No,' Jamie said through his teeth. 'I meant what Liz told you, before that happened.'

An icy whiteness filled her face. Appalled, she

whispered, 'Liz told . . . she told *you*?' For the second time that evening, Liz had stunned her. It was unbelievable that her cousin could have told Jamie Knox something so private, so embarrassing. Melanie felt as if the room dipped and swayed around her. She didn't understand anything tonight. She didn't understand anyone. If Liz had told a stranger what she had taken so long to tell Melanie herself, then Melanie did not know Liz any better than she knew Ross.

Jamie pushed his hands into his pockets, his tough body tensely poised. 'She needed to talk to someone. She was going quietly crazy. The first time I came here, when I brought you home, Liz and I had dinner and talked—maybe it was the wine or maybe Liz just couldn't keep it to herself any longer, but it came out.'

'She had no right,' Melanie burst out shakily. 'No right to tell you anything. It has nothing to do with you.' She hated the thought that he knew that her fiancé had made a pass at her cousin. How could Liz do it? How could she have told Jamie Knox a story like that?

'That hardly matters,' he said tersely, brushing her anger aside. 'The question is—what are you going to do about it?'

'You don't really think I'll discuss it with you, do you?' she muttered, turning away. He kept forcing himself into her life, trying to impose his views, his wishes, on her. The man was a menace, but he wasn't getting his own way this time. She wouldn't even let him mention it. She didn't want to know what he thought she should do, which was what he was obviously about to tell her. He could keep his opinions to himself. 'It's none of your damned business,' she broke out, shaking with anger.

He grabbed her shoulders, his fingers digging into her flesh, and forced her round towards him again.

'You aren't just going to bury it, forget she ever told you?'

'Let go of me!'

'You make me angry,' he said, as if he needed to tell her. 'It's as clear as daylight that your engagement is a farce.'

'You know nothing about it!'

'Don't I?' His mouth was hard and contemptuous and his dark eyes raked her face, making her flinch. 'It was obvious to me when we first met—you were upset because he'd gone off on business instead of keeping his promise to spend the weekend in the Lakes. No, you didn't say anything, but you didn't have to.'

'Oh, you can read my mind, I suppose?' she said bitterly, hating the way he stared at her.

'Yes, that's exactly it. I read your mind,' he said in an anger that matched hers. 'There's something else about Ross Ellis that you don't know, too.'

'I don't want to hear!' she said, struggling to get away. She had had enough for one night. She wanted no more shocks; she couldn't cope with any more revelations.

'Oh, I can see that!' he told her with a savage smile. 'But you're going to listen.'

'No, let go, stop it!' She hated the contempt she read in that strong face. What right did he have to despise her? What did he know about how she felt, what she thought? The only person who could see inside her heart was her, and even she didn't yet know exactly what she was going to do.

'You prefer to live in a fool's paradise than to face up to the truth?' he sneered angrily. 'It's so much cosier, isn't it? Ross Ellis is rich and important and all your friends will envy you when you're his wife. You'll have wardrobes of gorgeous clothes—a mink coat, Melanie? I'm sure you'd like a mink, girls usually do, don't they? Never mind the husband, look at the mink he'll give you? Isn't that what really matters to you? Oh, and Ross Ellis could give you one. Several, no doubt. He can give you most things money can buy. A grand house, a flashy car of your own, holidays in the South of France—or would you prefer Florida? Well, it doesn't matter, that's a minor detail. Wherever the jet set goes, you can go too—if you marry him. If you can stand being the discreet façade hiding a very empty private life, because you aren't in love with him, don't kid yourself you are, and he isn't in love with you, either.'

'Stop it, stop it,' she said frantically.

'Not until you've heard the truth! You won't be happy with him, you stupid girl. Can't you see that? His money won't help you to be happy.'

'I'm not interested in his money,' she spat out, trembling with an anger she couldn't control. She had never been interested in Ross's wealth, or his power in the business world; she had never looked past Ross himself to all the things which came with him. If he had been as rich as Croesus but unattractive to her, she wouldn't have seen him again, and she bitterly resented the accusations Jamie had just made.

Jamie's mouth twisted. 'No? Who are you trying to convince? Me? Or yourself?'

The top of her head seemed about to blow off. 'You?' she threw back at him hoarsely. 'You? I don't give a damn what you think, Mr Knox!'

Dark red rose in his face, his hands tightened on her slim shoulders until she winced.

'What on earth's going on?' said another voice from the doorway.

Melanie looked around and saw Liz staring at them with startled eyes.

'Haven't we had enough drama for one night?' Liz said, trying to laugh.

Melanie didn't smile back, she turned angry eyes on her cousin. 'You told him. You told him about Ross. How could you?' Her voice rose word by word, trembling with rage. 'Why not get a megaphone and tell the whole street? Print it in your damned paper, tell the world, why don't you? Liz, how could you?'

Liz seemed, for once, lost for words. She had flushed and her eyes moved to Jamie Knox's face, as if asking why he had told Melanie how indiscreet she had been. If Melanie had wondered if Jamie was telling the truth about hearing the story from Liz, she stopped wondering as she saw the look they exchanged. They didn't say a word, but their eyes talked, and watching that made Melanie angrier than ever.

'I'll never forgive you,' she told her cousin. 'Never.' She felt Jamie's grip on her slacken, and pulled away without so much as a look at him. Walking across the kitchen she passed Liz with one bitter glance, went through the hall, up the stairs to bed. Liz and Jamie could finish the clearing up. They could have one of their cosy, confidential chats while they did it, really let their hair down.

It was so unlike Liz. She had never been one for idle gossip and she didn't let just anybody into her confidence, but then if she had fallen in love with Jamie Knox he wouldn't be just anyone to her, would he? For Liz to open up with him like that, he had to be very special to her, and that meant it had to be serious, because Melanie couldn't remember the last time Liz had ever taken a man very seriously. Her relationships tended to be brittle, passing—men found her attractive but the type of men who fell for Liz were often shy and insecure which meant that Liz couldn't go for them, or they were sophisticated and often shallow which she certainly wasn't. Sophisticated, yes. Shallow, never. Liz wanted a very special man— not that she had told Melanie as much, but it was pretty obvious. The man Liz settled for would have to be someone as cool and aware as herself, yet inwardly as caring and capable of love.

The description didn't fit Jamie Knox, she thought coldly, as she undressed with shaky fingers and slid into bed. She didn't see him being capable of love. All evening he had flirted with her, hadn't he? Right under Liz's nose, too, although Liz hadn't seemed too worried by seeing them together, which was another puzzling feature of the whole evening.

The wind rattled the plywood boarding on her window, keeping her awake. She lay in the darkness, wishing she could stop her mind working. Will and Jamie had swept up all the glass and disposed of it. Her room looked spotless again, although the carpet was slightly damp where the rain had blown into the room. The only evidence of what had happened was the boarded window, and if they managed to get a glazier that, too, would have gone by the time Aunt Dolly and Uncle Teddy got back.

It wouldn't be as easy for her to erase all traces of the violence which had happened inside her tonight, though.

CHAPTER SIX

SHE slept very deeply, and very late into the morning woke up at the click of her door opening. Drowsily her lids lifted and she turned her dark head on the pillow, still half asleep.

When she saw Jamie she came awake in a hurry, clutching the sheet up to her chin. 'Get out of here! What do you think you're doing?'

'The glazier's downstairs,' he interrupted tersely.

Melanie drew breath. 'Oh.'

'Can you get up and dress quickly? I didn't expect him so soon or I'd have woken you earlier. I'm just going to make some coffee if you'd like to come down as soon as you're ready.'

The door closed and she stared at it, biting her lip, remembering everything that had happened last night, all the unpleasant, unjust things he had said to her. She hated him.

There was no point in lying there giving way to a brooding sense of the unfairness of fate for having brought Jamie Knox into her life, though, so she threw back the covers and swung out of bed, yawning. It was only then that she looked at the clock and saw that it was almost eleven o'clock in the morning.

On her way to the bathroom she saw that both Will and Liz had their doors shut; the sound of their slow breathing came through the wood very audibly. They were still asleep. They wouldn't stay that way once the glazier got to work, though.

A quick shower helped Melanie to come fully awake. Returning to her room in her brief terry robe, she met Jamie on the landing, his face thunderous.

'How much longer are you going to be? I've had to make the guy some breakfast now, or he'd have left without doing the job.'

'I'll be five minutes,' she said, trying not to notice the way his eyes explored the deep plunge between the lapels of her robe, the bare damp legs below the hem of it.

Jamie held up his wrist, tapping his watch. 'Five minutes—I'm timing you.'

'Oh, get lost,' Melanie said, furious, and dived back into her room, but she dressed rapidly in the first thing that came to hand—snug-fitting white denims and a sky-blue cotton top with a demure, scooped neckline. Her mirror showed her a neat reflection. She stared at it grimly. She looked like a schoolgirl. Well, why not? At least that might make Jamie Knox keep his distance, so she tied her black hair into two curling bunches, with blue satin bows, to complete the image. Let him come a foot too close today and she would hit him with something.

When she got down to the kitchen Jamie looked pointedly at his watch. 'Seven minutes precisely,' he said, but Melanie pretended not to have heard that.

A grey-haired workman in well-washed blue dungarees sat at the kitchen table finishing bacon, egg and toast. Picking up a cup of increadibly strong tea, he nodded to her. 'Sorry to get you out of bed in a hurry, miss, but I'm a bit pushed for time.'

Melanie smiled at him. 'That's okay, I'm glad to

see you—we're very keen to get the window done before my uncle and aunt get back.'

'So I heard. I don't know what these kids are coming to—chucking stones through windows because they were thrown out of a party. As if I didn't have enough to do, and this a Saturday too.' The workman drained his cup, got up and picked up his bag of tools. 'Well, I'll go up and get to work, if you'll show me the way, Mr Knox.'

Melanie cleared the table and made herself some toast and a boiled egg. She was eating it when Jamie came back.

'You may be interested to hear that our glazier thought you were still at school,' he drawled, sitting down at the table too and stretching his long legs with a sigh. 'It's the hairstyle, makes you look about fifteen.'

Melanie drank some coffee, her eyes lowered. How much longer was he going to stay? Why didn't he go home now?

'But then that was the idea, wasn't it? They call it regression—a deliberate retreat into childhood. Makes it easier to ignore problems the patient can't face.' Jamie paused, as if waiting for her to defend herself, but she went on ignoring him.

'At a guess I'd say that that's why you went for Ross Ellis, too,' he went on, when he saw she wasn't rising to his bait. 'Does he realise he's just your security blanket, I wonder?'

Melanie blazed into open rage at that, her dark blue eyes hating him. 'Why don't you leave me alone?'

He linked his hands behind his head, lying back in the chair in an attitude of casual mockery. 'Why, Melanie? Am I actually getting through to you, is that what worries you?'

'Don't kid yourself,' she spat, glaring. 'I'm sick

of being a target for your bullets, that's all. So why don't you get back into that showy car of yours and go home? Go away, stay away.'

'You're losing your temper,' he taunted softly. 'You don't want to do that, Melanie, do you? Any sort of real emotion threatens that dream world you've gone to such trouble to build up. If you actually started to think about how you really *feel* you might not be able to go through with marrying Ellis, and that would never do, would it? All that cosy security gone! What might happen to you then?'

Melanie got stumblingly to her feet, trembling with fury, but before she had thrown something at Jamie or hit him or screamed, the doorbell went sharply and she regained control of herself enough to walk past Jamie down the hall to the front door.

When she saw Ross standing there she stared blankly at him for a second, almost shocked by the sight of him. He was casually dressed today; pale grey trousers, a fine slate-coloured cashmere sweater, over which he wore a blue leather jacket. Even in such casual clothes he managed to look very elegant and stylish.

'Ross! You're back, then—I'd been waiting for you to ring.'

'I came, instead.' He kissed her lightly and offered her a large gold, ribbon-tied box. 'I bought you some real Turkish Delight in a bazaar in Bahrain.'

'Oh, how nice,' Melanie said, hoping Jamie wouldn't come out into the hall. She was appalled by the prospect of a meeting between the two men, but how could she get out of it? 'Come into the drawing-room,' she stammered, wondering if Jamie had heard them talking.

Ross was observing her childish hairstyle and

clean-scrubbed face with faint surprise. 'You look very sweet today.'

'Thank you,' she said uneasily, afraid of actually hustling him out of the hall but still hoping to avert a meeting with Jamie. 'Did you have a successful trip, Ross?'

'I managed to pull the chestnuts out of the fire,' he said. 'Did you go to the Lakes? I'm sorry I couldn't make it, Melanie, but I hope you went and enjoyed yourself.'

She steered him into the drawing-room, hoping it was now reasonably tidy. Darting a look around it she saw with relief that Jamie and Liz must have spent some time on restoring it to normal. Nothing now seemed out of place.

'Yes, I went, and did some sailing and climbing,' she admitted, as the glazier began hammering upstairs. Ross lifted his eyes to the ceiling, his expression quizzical.

'What's going on in your bedroom? I saw one of your windows was broken.' He listened smilingly as Melanie began to tell him about Will's birthday party.

'And I forgot all about it! I'm sorry, my mind was otherwise occupied. I'd meant to get him a present—never mind, I'll remember to get him something tomorrow.' Then he smiled. 'It must have been a good party if windows got broken, though.'

She told him what had happened and he frowned, asking quickly, 'You weren't hurt?'

'No, just shaken.'

'And Liz?'

'She didn't even realise it had happened until Will told her.'

The sunlight streaming in through the high windows showed her the pale gold of his hair and, for the first time, a faint silvering of the immaculate strands. Perhaps it was because Ross was looking tired; his week of intensive negotiations in Bahrain had taken its toll. He looked older, faintly weary.

'Was your trip exhausting, Ross?' she asked gently, and he shrugged.

'The heat sapped my energy, I could never live in a climate like that. Even with air-conditioning in my hotel I found myself having to take cool showers several times a day, and when you were out on the site itself, you had a problem with the flies and sand and dirt. My throat was so dry all the time that I had a sore throat within two days. It was a useful exercise to go out there myself because I had a better idea why the men were causing so much trouble. Once I could see it from their angle, I knew how to solve the problem.'

'When did you actually get back?'

'Yesterday, but I had to see the other directors and explain what arrangments I'd made and by then it was too late to get in touch with you.'

They were talking like strangers, Melanie thought bleakly, as she nodded. That was what they were, though, wasn't it? Ross never really took her into his confidence, he didn't treat her as an equal, talk about what was worrying him, ask her advice or help. How did he think about her? Or didn't he think about her at all, apart from remembering to buy her a box of sweets before returning from this business trip?

Well, they had to talk and soon, because it couldn't go on like this—Jamie Knox was right, although she would die rather than admit as much to him. This wasn't the time or the place, however. At any minute Jamie might wander in and overhear them.

'I thought we might have lunch out somewhere,'

Ross murmured. 'Or have you made other arrangements?'

So polite, she thought, looking at him wryly. In his presence she found it even more incredible that he had made a pass at Liz, or that he was in the habit of making passes at any women. When she heard Liz telling that story she had believed it because she couldn't remember Liz lying to her before, but now, looking at Ross, her belief faltered and fragmented. There was something so out of character about the thought of Ross behaving like that. It didn't add up. Yet Liz simply didn't lie, so he must have made a pass at her. Had he been drunk? She hadn't noticed that, and she remembered vaguely that he had taken her home after that party. She was sure he had been sober; in fact, he'd been rather quiet and withdrawn for most of the evening. Melanie's bewilderment only deepened further the more she tried to work out the truth, tried to make sense of the puzzle. The pieces didn't fit together, which could only mean that there was a piece of the jigsaw missing.

Jamie Knox might mock her and say that she didn't know Ross at all and didn't understand him, but Jamie Knox was wrong in one sense—she understood what she knew about Ross, she couldn't believe he was the sort of man Liz and Jamie seemed to think he was and her own judgment of people wasn't as blinkered as Jamie imagined. It was Jamie who was looking at Ross from the wrong angle, not her.

'Lunch would be very nice,' she said slowly, and Ross looked at his watch.

'Good, and there's plenty of time for you to change.'

That was his only reference, gently indulgent, to

her neat schoolgirl appearance, and Melanie grimaced.

'Yes, I won't be very long. Do sit down, Ross. Would you like some coffee while you wait?'

'That would be very welcome,' he said in his calm, tired voice, taking off his leather jacket and folding it neatly over the back of a chair before he sat down on the couch.

Jamie was in the kitchen drinking black coffee, but if Melanie had hoped that he hadn't realised who had arrived she soon found she was wrong.

'He timed his arrival nicely,' he said, leaning against the draining-board, his mug in one hand, watching Melanie start to make a pot of coffee for Ross. 'Were his ears burning? I'm ready to bet you didn't tell him we'd been talking about him when he arrived.'

She hunted for a cup and saucer from Aunt Dolly's best coffee-service, a silver wedding anniversary present from Liz to her parents several years ago. Aunt Dolly rarely used the pretty bone china with its silver stripe and faint pink rosebuds. She liked to look at it in her china cabinet but was afraid it might get broken if it was actually used.

'It's madness, you know that, don't you?' Jamie said as she set out the silver tray. 'His money won't make you happy, Melanie. It's all an illusion. Wake up before it's too late.'

She filled the cream-jug and the silver sugar-bowl which matched the tray, still ignoring Jamie.

'Nothing but the best for Ross Ellis,' Jamie murmured with dry impatience a moment later. 'Can't you see that you'll be stifled by the way he lives? Look at you now—if you were making that coffee for me you'd make instant coffee in a mug and hand it to me. But for him it has to be all the frills. He expects it and he gets it, doesn't he?

That's not the life you're used to. Oh, no doubt you find it exciting, moving in that world for the first time, but when the novelty wears off and you realise you've married a man you don't love, who doesn't love you, all the glitter and frills in this world won't help you, Melanie.'

'Who the hell do you think you are?' Melanie erupted, turning on him at last with a flushed and agitated face. 'You hardly know me. You can't guess whether I love Ross or not.'

'You don't,' he stated with cool certainty.

'Don't say that!' Melanie seethed, dying to hit him with something. 'You know nothing about it.'

'I saw the two of you together just now in the hall. I saw the way he kissed you. It wasn't exactly earth-shattering, was it? You didn't run into each other's arms. In fact, you sounded like a couple of bored strangers making polite conversation.' He imitated her, his eyes mocking. 'Did you have a successful trip, Ross?' His mouth twisted derisively. 'As for him, I should think he makes more show of being pleased to see his dog.' He imitated Ross's calm, quiet voice. 'You look very sweet.' Jamie's face was scornful. 'Sweet! My God!'

The coffee was beginning to bubble against the glass dome. Melanie felt rather like that, too; fury was boiling inside her and she was tempted to explode in Jamie's face, but she was afraid of what that might precipitate, she had a distinct suspicion that Jamie was determined to provoke some reaction out of her and that she wouldn't enjoy whatever he planned to do next.

'All men aren't like you,' she said instead, keeping her rage suppressed but making her voice icily contemptuous.

He flicked a glance at her through his lashes. 'So you've noticed that, at last.'

She was disturbed by the gleam in those dark eyes. 'It wasn't meant as a compliment!' she denied.

'All the same, it is one,' mocked Jamie, his smile maddeningly self-satisfied. 'And for the record, the last word I'd apply to you is sweet . . . you're about as sweet as poison ivy. Every time I'm anywhere near you I get some dangerous symptoms.'

The coffee was ready; Melanie darted to switch it off, averting her flushed face from him. 'Thanks,' she bit out, putting the coffee-pot on the tray. 'I'm very flattered.'

He laughed as she walked to the door. 'But you'll notice that I keep coming back,' he said softly.

She didn't look round or admit she had heard that. Her throat was hot and dry and she felt strangely miserable. What did he mean by that? Or was it just empty words? Jamie Knox flirted easily with every girl he met, he had taken Liz out to dinner the first time he came here and Liz was by no means an easy pick-up. She had pretty high standards where men were concerned; she didn't fall for any man who looked twice at her.

She carried the tray into the drawing-room and poured Ross a cup of coffee. He was leaning back in the chair, his eyes closed, when she came into the room and opened them slowly to smile at her in that tired way.

'Everyone else out?' he asked casually.

'Liz and Will aren't up yet, but I expect the glazier has woken them by now. He's making quite a noise, isn't he?' The man was chipping all the broken glass out of the frame now.

Leaving Ross sipping his coffee, Melanie went up to her bedroom. The glazier turned his head and grinned. 'I'll be quite a time yet, miss, I'm afraid.'

'That's all right—I'm going out, anyway.' Melanie collected some clothes and went into the bathroom to change. A few moments later someone rattled the doorhandle.

'I'm in here—I'll be out in five minutes,' called Melanie.

'Melly? You pest,' Liz said with a yawn. 'My head is hammering.'

'That's the glazier in my room,' Melanie said, smiling, as she eyed her reflection in the bathroom mirror. She had put on a turquoise shift dress, pure silk, very simple and smooth-fitting. She began lightly brushing her hair into its customary soft style, curved inward around her face, framing it elegantly.

'Glazier? He got here quickly.' Liz pattered away, yawning again.

Melanie did her make-up without haste, using very little because her skin looked better without too much. Her mirror now showed her a very different image—cool, slender and composed, a girl who had herself and her life very much under control. She considered the reflection wryly; it was a lie, of course, an illusion she had conjured up with cosmetics and clothes, but knowing that she gave that impression would make it easier for her to talk to Ross.

She didn't yet know how to introduce the subject; she would have to play it by ear, wait for the right moment. Jamie Knox might imagine that he had prodded her into looking twice at her engagement, but he was wrong. The morning she drove off to the Lakes alone she had been poised on the edge of realising she had made a mistake; Jamie's interference had only accelerated a process which had begun before he met her.

Her blue eyes flashed as she remembered Jamie's insulting suggestion that she was marrying Ross for his money. He'd made her very angry when he said that, but she could brush the insult aside because she knew it wasn't true. Ross's money meant nothing to her. It wasn't as simple, though, to shrug off the accusation that she was clinging to Ross for emotional security, and she frowned at her reflection as if her eyes betrayed something disastrous.

Ross was a strong man, comfortingly assured. She had found a kind of peace with him at first; had it been a false peace? Much as she loved her uncle and aunt, and both her cousins, she had never felt she belonged with them in quite the way she had with her parents. It wasn't easy to put into words, or even think about; it was more a matter of instinct and intuition than logic. Looking back to her childhood she saw it as a golden warmth, like a summer day: confident, stable. Yes, secure— Jamie was right, damn him. However hard Aunt Dolly and Uncle Teddy tried, they could never take the place of her parents. There was always that something missing, indefinable but unforgotten. When Ross asked her to marry him that special feeling of belonging had seemed to shimmer ahead like a mirage in a desert and she had eagerly run to find it.

Perhaps she would, some day—but not with Ross, and she had come to see that long before Jamie Knox started making his derisive comments. She might have faced the truth sooner if she didn't feel a tremor of regret every time she thought of saying goodbye to that hope of love and security in a family again. Was that what people meant when

they talked of falling in love with love? The state
of being in love was so wonderful it was easy to
deceive yourself.

She grimaced, turning away. The longer she left
Ross alone the more chance there was of Jamie
talking to him, saying something that might
precipitate a crisis Melanie wasn't ready to face
yet.

She came down the stairs just in time to see Liz
in her old rose-pink velvet housecoat wandering
across the hall. Liz paused at the open door of the
drawing-room, glancing into the room.

Melanie saw her face in profile; saw the smooth
skin tighten over Liz's cheekbones, a hot wave of
colour flow up to her hairline.

It was rare for Liz to look so shaken; it wasn't
easy to throw her off balance, but Melanie saw it
happen now, and paused on the stairs, her mind
working like lightning, putting two and two together
with a rapidity that shook her as deeply as Liz was
visibly shaken.

'Oh, hallo,' Liz said in an abrupt, deep voice.

Melanie couldn't see Ross but she knew that Liz
was speaking to him.

'Hallo,' Ross said, and the sound of his voice
made Melanie's eyes widen.

There was a strange little silence, then Liz said
huskily, 'Does Melanie know you're here?'

'Yes,' he said, his voice becoming brusque.

'Oh, well . . .' Liz backed. Melanie saw her hand
catch hold of the wall; the skin was stretched tautly
over the white knuckles. 'Well, she won't be long,'
Liz said. 'Excuse me.'

Melanie felt horribly out of place, she would
have backed out of sight if she could have done so
without drawing attention to her presence, but Liz
didn't look up or notice her. She walked unsteadily

towards the kitchen, the door opened and closed and Melanie stared at it fixedly.

How could I be so blind for so long? she thought.

CHAPTER SEVEN

THE shock of her new suspicions absorbed so much of her attention that she let Ross put her into the passenger seat of his Rolls, slide in beside her behind the driving wheel and turn south out of Carlisle heading for Kendal without Melanie noticing the direction he had taken, or being aware of anything much except her own thoughts.

Her immediate reaction was to think that Liz had, after all, lied to her, but it slowly dawned on her that Liz hadn't lied so much as suppressed her own side of the story. Liz hadn't wanted to admit she was attracted to Ross; and why should she? It was a complication that Liz felt had nothing to do with the matter. Melanie knew her cousin well enough, and had noticed enough of her manner whenever Ross was around to be certain that Liz had not given him a hint how she felt. Far from it, Liz had frozen when she saw him. She must have gone to great lengths to make sure that Ross never suspected her real feelings, because Melanie had been totally deceived. She had been sure that Liz disliked Ross, and she thought Ross had believed that, too.

When Ross, nevertheless, made a pass at her, Liz would have been doubly shaken—on her own behalf as well as on Melanie's. Her mind must have been in turmoil, wondering if she had betrayed her feelings, terrified of admitting them, filled with guilt. Hadn't she said as much? She had skated over the reasons for her sense of guilt, but Melanie vividly recalled her cousin's face. Liz had been more upset than angry—Melanie should have guessed at once that her cousin was withholding something for Liz had been far too distressed for it to be mere sympathy for Melanie.

Melanie had only a hazy memory of that party which had been so traumatic for Liz. For her it had been just another night, one she had more or less forgotten almost at once. Wasn't it odd how one event could seem so different from other angles?

'I thought we'd eat by the river in Kendal, that restaurant we've been to before,' Ross said abruptly.

Looking round with a start, she said, 'Oh, yes, I remember—that will be nice. The place with the lovely view of the river?' He had taken her there several times. The restaurant was on the upper floor, its bar looked down over the river so that one could drink and watch the current flowing darkly under an old bridge.

'The food is good, too,' Ross said with a brief smile before switching his gaze to the motorway ahead. What was he thinking? Were their thoughts running on the same theme? She suspected that they were.

Why had he ever asked her to marry him? An impulse decision? They had met so casually, but Ross must have realised at once that he had bowled her off her feet. She had only been out with boys of her own age until then, and Ross was used to dating far more sophisticated women. Had it been Melanie's wide-eyed and dazzled gaze that had given him the idea of marrying her? Had he only proposed after he had begun to think she was in love with him?

A flush crept up her cheeks as it dawned on her

that she, herself, might have unknowingly brought about the proposal which had been such a surprise at the time. They had both been under a flattering spell, of course; she had been amazed at interest from a man like Ross and he, in turn, had been touched by her shy reactions to him.

But he hadn't met Liz until after he proposed, had he? Up to that time, their dates had been on neutral ground, like the restaurant to which he was taking her now. When had he begun to realise how he felt about Liz? Was it an instant attraction? Or did it grow gradually?

Looking slowly back over the months, Melanie felt sure that Ross had finally understood his own feelings on the night of Brenda's party. It was after that that his attitude had changed, that he began to be distant and suddenly far too busy to see her.

Or was she deluding herself? Had something been going on between Liz and Ross all these months?

She looked sharply at him, searching his features—no, she couldn't believe that, about either of them.

Ross sensed her gaze and turned his head. 'Sorry to be abstracted,' he said politely. 'I've got something on my mind.'

Melanie watched him, stiffening. 'Would it help to talk about it?'

The calm façade of his face seemed to crack; she caught a glimpse of confused emotions in his eyes, on his parted mouth. She took an expectant breath—one of them had to make the first move to unravel the tangle into which their lives had been scrambled. Was that what he was thinking? Was he going to say something at last?

But he looked away with a deep sigh. 'No, I don't think so.'

Melanie bit her lip. The day he left for Bahrain she had told him that she simply didn't feel she knew him well enough to marry him. She had left out some of what she wanted to say; her uncertainty had been too vague, too indefinable—a muddled suspicion that she wasn't really in love with him? Or just an instinctive awareness that they were both making a mistake? She hadn't seen him again until today, they still hadn't talked frankly, yet she felt, oddly, that she had begun to learn a lot more about him in his absence, and she felt a distinct prickle of pity for him.

It surprised her because pity wasn't an emotion she had ever expected to feel for Ross, he wasn't a man one would imagine ever needing it, but, watching his tense profile, compassion was what she did feel. Ross was trapped and unhappy. Did he suspect how Liz felt about him? Or did he think that his feelings were not returned? Liz had been so angry when she talked about Ross that Melanie was sure that Liz didn't realise that Ross was seriously attracted to her; she had put his pass down to something very different. She had been hurt, humiliated, distressed by that moment on the roof garden of Brenda's flat. It had made her think that Ross was promiscuous and a flirt, without scruples, and Liz had hardened towards him after that. Melanie had picked up anger and pain in her voice when she stood in the doorway of the drawing-room looking at Ross. Poor Liz, she thought, frowning.

Suddenly it occurred to her that she might be in a better position to understand Liz and Ross than they could yet understand themselves—or each other.

It was a weird sort of irony. She was the third point of their triangle; from her angle she could

see them clearly now, she was convinced of that.
Each of them might imagine they could see her,
but they simply didn't see each other. They were
both too busy hiding how they felt, and in assuming
those disguises they not only hid from each other,
they no longer saw her, at all; they saw the image
of her they had invented.

She watched Ross through lowered lashes, face
thoughtful. He thought she was in love with him,
didn't he? He was afraid of hurting her by telling
her the truth. And Liz's feelings were even more
complex because she would never take Melanie's
man away from her knowingly, yet at the same
time she had got the impression that Ross was a
worthless flirt and not good enough for her cousin.

No wonder she was in such a state after she told
me about the pass he had made at her! Again she
thought: poor Liz!

The sun gleamed on the fells, glinted on the
slates of Kendal as they approached the town.
Ross seemed to have nothing to say, brooding in
silence as he began looking for a parking place
close to the riverside restaurant.

They were the first customers to arrive; the
restaurant had just opened and the place was
empty. They were able to get a good table by the
window in the bar and the waiter immediately
brought them menus and asked what they would
like to drink. Melanie ordered a Snowball; Ross
asked for Scotch on the rocks.

'I didn't touch a drink while I was in Bahrain,'
he said, grimacing. 'It's quite a relief to get back
home. I'm only just beginning to get the taste of
sand out of my mouth.'

Considering him, she noticed the sunburn flush
on his nose and cheeks. 'You caught the sun.'

'Unavoidably,' he murmured. 'The minute you

get off the plane it beats on your head like a gong. How was the weather in the Lakes?'

'Changeable.' She met his eyes. 'Ross, before you went to Bahrain I tried to talk to you about our engagement . . .'

'I remember,' he said, his face wary.

'Can we talk about it now?'

He looked away from her at the sunlit, flowing river. 'You said something about not feeling you knew me well enough to marry me.'

'Yes.'

His face was expressionless. What was he thinking? She had a spasm of impatience with him—was he going to let her do all the work? Couldn't he see how difficult it was for her to break their engagement without giving a reason? Or did he believe that she had a reason in his own behaviour, the distance he had put between them over the last few months? Ross wasn't the type to find it easy to pretend, to act a part he no longer felt. If he regretted asking her to marry him yet couldn't bring himself to admit as much, he might be sitting there now hoping that she would do all the difficult work for him. She couldn't decide whether that was cowardice or kindness; whatever it was, it made it hard for her.

'We got engaged so fast,' she said. 'We hardly knew each other.'

The waiter appeared again and she bit down on her inner lip. Ross didn't betray any impatience by so much as a flicker. He glanced at her politely.

'Ready to order?'

Melanie ordered a simple meal—iced melon and salmon mayonnaise. Ross had the melon, too, and then a rare steak. He ordered a wine he knew she liked and the waiter took the menus and vanished. Some more guests were arriving, local businessmen in sober suits who paused to inspect the cold buffet table in the centre of the room before clustering around the bar to order drinks. The restaurant was filling up, and she would have to talk in a lower voice unless she wanted to be overheard.

Ross drank some of his Scotch, then said, 'What do you want to do about it?'

For a second Melanie didn't realise what he meant, she looked at him blankly, then flushed. 'Oh . . . well . . . don't you think we should put off any talk of marriage, Ross? I mean . . .' Her mind was suddenly confused, she didn't know what she had meant.

'Postpone our marriage, you mean?' Ross suggested evenly, watching her.

How could you ask a man you were two months away from marrying if he really loved you? It wouldn't be so hard if she knew for certain that his answer would be no. That would make it all simple. But what if he looked her in the eye and said that of course he loved her. What did she do then?

When she didn't answer, Ross said in the same calm voice, 'Of course we can, if that is what you want. There's no rush. Take all the time you need to think it over.'

She picked up her glass and drank some of the yellow foamy drink, trying to work out how to answer. She hadn't intended a postponement; she had meant to give him back his ring and end their engagement altogether, but Ross had made that impossible.

A bewildered qualm hit her—had she read the situation wrongly? Had she jumped to crazy conclusions about how he and Liz felt? Was Ross still serious about wanting to marry her, after all?

She turned and watched the shadows under the

bridge; sleek and dark in motion, the water surged into them until she couldn't see it any more.

Anxiety tightened her stomach. Whatever Ross really felt, she knew that she did not love him. The certainty was as cold as lead inside her. The dazzled excitement of her first weeks of knowing him had faded, long ago. She wasn't in love with him but she liked him too much to risk hurting him if she was wrong about how he felt.

The waiter came over, smiling. 'Your table is ready when you are, sir.'

'Are we ready?' Ross asked her politely.

She nodded, getting up, and they followed the man across the restaurant towards a table for two by the window on the far side. Suddenly Melanie heard Ross draw a thick breath, stiffening. Puzzled, she glanced up at him. He was staring towards the door, a dark wash of colour flowing up his face.

Melanie followed his stare and her own nerves jumped as she saw Liz walking towards them with Jamie Knox.

'What the hell is Knox doing with Liz?' Ross muttered.

Melanie's dark blue eyes widened until her skin stretched painfully. Ross must have heard her gasp because he looked down at her, frowning.

'You know him?' she said incredulously. Jamie hadn't mentioned ever meeting Ross.

'We've met,' Ross said curtly. 'How do you and Liz come to know him?'

Before she could answer the other two were in earshot and Ross shot them a hard stare.

Liz looked sleekly elegant in a burnt-orange jersey dress which Melanie had never seen her wear before, it must be new.

Summoning a smile, Melanie said, 'Hallo, fancy seeing you here!'

'It's a small world,' Liz said coolly, but the brown eyes that met Melanie's held a glint of defiance. Was it pure coincidence that she and Jamie had turned up? Yet how could they possibly have known that Ross would bring her here? And why should they follow them, anyway?

'You look very chic—I haven't seen that dress before,' said Melanie, her eyes questioning.

Liz gave a wry little grin. 'That's because it's new—I only bought it this morning, and Jamie decided it deserved to go somewhere special.'

The two men were eyeing each other without any pretence of cordiality.

Ross nodded curtly. 'Knox!'

Jamie's smile held cold mockery. 'Ellis.' His tone deliberately mimicked Ross.

Melanie stared pointedly at Jamie—why hadn't he told her that he actually knew Ross? They had talked enough about him, heaven knew, so why had Jamie been so secretive?

He slid a sideways look at her, his dark eyes glinting, as if her astonishment and annoyance amused him. He had changed, too; he was wearing a crisp red and white striped shirt and a dark red silk tie. His suit was dark grey and made him seem taller, but it couldn't tame the wildness of those black eyes and the thick black hair. Even in these civilised and formal surroundings Jamie Knox carried an air of danger with him like private oxygen.

The waiter hovered politely, Ross glanced at him then said, 'I'm afraid we have to go—our table's ready.'

'See you later,' Jamie said drily, not to him, but to Melanie, who looked back at him without warmth. When she got a chance she was going to make him explain why he hadn't told her he knew Ross.

She sat down at the table, the waiter deftly laid her napkin across her lap with a faintly theatrical gesture, and a moment later the melon arrived and she and Ross began to eat.

'How long have you known Knox?' he asked her, his fair head bent. She looked uneasily at him.

'Oh, not long. I met him at Ullswater.'

He looked up. 'Last weekend?'

She nodded and ate some more of the cool, greeny-yellow melon; the refreshing taste did little to calm her overheated nerves. She hadn't looked towards the bar but she was aware of Liz and Jamie in there, drinking champagne—she had heard the little explosion of the cork coming out, Liz laughing. What were they celebrating? she wondered edgily.

Ross was frowning. 'And Liz? When did she meet him?'

'The same weekend.' Melanie wondered if she ought to tell him now that she had spent a night marooned in an isolated hut on the fells with Jamie Knox. Somehow she couldn't; if it had seemed fraught with difficulties at first, such a confession now would be ten times harder, because Ross very obviously did not like Jamie, and the feeling was clearly mutual. Jamie did not like him.

Ross looked towards the bar. 'He's a fast worker.' It was said with cold anger and Melanie followed his gaze. Jamie faced her, a glass of champagne in his hand. He raised it mockingly, smiling, and Melanie looked away.

'Yes, isn't he?' she said. Ross didn't know how fast or how unscrupulous.

Ross shot her a probing look. 'What do you know about him?'

Startled, she shook her head. 'Nothing much—he lives at Ullswater, he has a red sports-car and at the moment he hasn't got a job.'

Ross smiled tightly. 'Because I sacked him,' he said and Melanie almost choked on her melon. Coughing, she reached for her glass of white wine and drank a little. When she could speak again she asked, 'What did you say?'

'He used to work for me,' Ross repeated. 'He's a brilliant engineer, I certainly couldn't fault his work, but we didn't see eye to eye about certain things, so he had to go.'

Staring at him, Melanie asked, 'What didn't you see eye to eye about?'

Ross frowned. 'We were offered a huge contract by a certain country. Knox felt we shouldn't sign it; he disliked the government in question. He was entitled to his opinion, that wasn't why I sacked him—but he went too far, he tried to drum up support among members of my board, sent each of them a letter giving his views in rather lurid language. There was a good deal of trouble and several directors came out in his support. I couldn't sign the contract while the board was split like that, but before I could talk them round it got to the ears of the other people; they were very offended and withdrew the contract altogether.' He finished his melon and flung down his table napkin with an angry gesture. 'Knox cost the company millions of pounds. When his contract came up for renewal at the end of the year, I didn't take it up.'

'He didn't tell us anything about that,' Melanie said slowly. Or had he told Liz? They seemed to have become very confidential in a very short time. Liz had told him that Ross had made a pass at her.

Had she told Jamie because he had just told her why Ross had fired him?

'You don't surprise me. Knox is mischievous and irresponsible.'

Melanie stared at Ross, her dark blue eyes sombre. When she realised that he and Jamie knew each other, she had thought at first that Jamie hadn't told her because he was being mischievous, but his reason for silence had been rather more worrying. Jamie had a grudge against Ross; bitterly disliked him. He had wilfully misled her—why? Had he planned to use her as some sort of weapon in a revenge on Ross?

The waiter removed their plates and began to serve their main course, so for a while they hardly said anything.

Melanie ate her cold salmon and creamy mayonnaise without really tasting either; she left just under half of the meal, pushing the food around her plate idly, her mind angrily busy.

Once when she looked up she found Ross watching Liz and Jamie being shown to their table on the other side of the room. Ross looked grim, his grey eyes shadowed.

Melanie wished she could be sure what she was seeing—she no longer felt able to guess at anybody's motives, anybody's real feelings. There was no solid ground under her feet. Her ears beat with hypertension and her mind kept dissolving into endless, unanswered questions.

It seemed that Ross had some questions of his own. Leaning forward he asked abruptly, 'You didn't say how you came to meet Knox at Ullswater.'

Melanie hesitated, but she was so sick of hiding things, keeping back the full truth.

'I went fell climbing while I was there and got

trapped in heavy mist. He came to find me. We couldn't get down again, you couldn't see a yard ahead, so we had to spend the night in a hut up there.'

Ross sat there staring. 'Alone?'

She swallowed, nodding.

Ross held her eyes, his face hard. 'I see.'

'I doubt if I'd have found it on my own,' Melanie stammered. 'The hut, I mean. I vaguely knew there was one but in that mist . . . and I'd hurt my ankle, I could only hobble. He was a real survival expert; I was very grateful for his help. He made a fire and found straw to sleep on and he . . .' Her voice trailed off. 'He may not actually have saved my life. I don't think it was ever in danger. But all the same, I was very glad he was there.' Even to please and placate Ross she wasn't going to lie about that. Whatever Jamie's reasons for coming to find her—and she strongly suspected them now—she had to be grateful for what he had done for her.

'Of course,' Ross said, but those cool grey eyes asked other questions which she certainly couldn't answer, because even to admit she knew what was in his mind would be some sort of admission. Not of guilt, necesssarily, but of awareness. Jamie hadn't tried to make love to her that night. She could look Ross in the eye and tell him so truthfully. But something serious had happened while they were alone in the mist and rain, and that she could not talk to Ross about. Jamie Knox had got under her skin; he was there now, needling, infuriating, tormenting, driving her crazy.

Ross looked down, his brows level, then looked up again. 'Were your aunt and uncle worried?' The question was casual but his eyes were far from casual, and she couldn't meet them.

'They only heard about it when I got back safely.'

'And how did they react to the news that you'd spent a night alone with Knox?' Ross murmured, pushing his own reactions on to Aunt Dolly and Uncle Teddy.

She forced a smile; at least that made it easier for her to answer.

'Oh, they didn't get over-excited. They know me; I'm not stupid.'

'I wouldn't have thought Liz was stupid, either.' Ross said, glowering across the room at that other table. Jamie and Liz were just getting lobster Thermidor and were laughing like a couple of children. The sight of their enjoyment didn't seem to delight Ross, and it didn't do much for Melanie either. She felt stupidly excluded, shut out, watching them through a window. A glance at Ross made her supect that he felt the same.

'Ross,' she said.

He didn't take his eyes from the other two. 'Mmm?'

'We're not in love, are we?' she said gently.

That caught his attention, his head swung and he stared at her fixedly, turning dark red. 'What?'

Melanie gave him a wry, melancholy little smile. 'It was a mistake, wasn't it, for both of us?'

Ross swallowed, his throat moving convulsively, but he seemed struck dumb. She held his eyes, reading relief in them. The barrier that had hidden his real thoughts and feelings from her for months had gone. Ross watched her nod, still smiling.

'You should have said something. We might have gone ahead and got married and then we'd be in a mess,' she said.

Ross gave a sudden deep laugh, his hand moving over the table to take hers and hold it tightly.

'Melanie . . . what can I say?'

'Try the truth. I'd welcome it,' Melanie told him softly.

The flush on his face increased. 'I didn't want to hurt you, Melanie.'

'I know and I'm not. It dawned on me too, gradually.'

'Why didn't *you* say something long ago?'

'I'm a slow thinker,' she said, and he laughed.

'I don't believe it.' Then he stopped laughing and looked hard at her. 'You mean it? You really aren't hurt? I was afraid . . .'

'That you'd have to marry me, after all?' she teased. 'No, Ross, you can breathe again.'

He still looked concerned, uncertain, watching her intently. 'You aren't just saying this because you think . . . because you suspect I . . .'

'I'm saying it because I mean it, Ross. I'm very fond of you. I like you very much but I'm not in love with you. For a while I thought I was.'

'Yes, *I* thought *I* was!' he said quickly. 'You're so sweet and easy to love, Melanie. You're a very gentle person—maybe that's why I thought you were the wife I wanted. I'm not gentle. I'm afraid I'm far from gentle. In my world that's the last quality that's needed. I'm successful because I'm naturally tough. I've had to be. Throw me against a brick wall and I'd bounce.' He laughed shortly. 'Someone said that to me once, and he didn't mean it as a compliment.' He looked at her, grimacing.

'Jamie Knox?' she guessed, from his expression.

'Bull's eye. Jamie Knox.' Ross's upper lip curled angrily.

'I shouldn't let his remarks sting,' Melanie said in hidden irony at her own expense. She had let Jamie Knox's words sting her far too often; never again. 'He's not worth bothering about,' she added, and Ross shrugged.

'He had something that time, though. 'I've had to fight to get to the top of my business and I'd begun to feel it was time to relax, enjoy myself more, build some sort of private life for myself. I met you and you seemed purpose-built for me—exactly the sort of girl I'd had in mind.'

She looked startled and a little shocked, and Ross noticed that and gave her an apologetic smile.

'I know. It sounds like computerised dating, but I didn't stop to take a good look at how I was acting. I've got so used to seeing something I want, something I've had in mind, a big contract or a firm that might be useful to me, and just moving in on it fast and buying it up before anyone else can get to it first. That's business today, Melanie. You can't play gentlemanly games. You have to grab. So . . .'

'You grabbed me?'

'I'm sorry.'

'And then you realised you didn't want me after all?' She was glad she had realised she wasn't in love with him before she actually started to hear all this. If she had been emotionally involved it would have hurt to hear herself talked about with this ruthless neutrality, as a piece of property he had thought valuable but now no longer wanted.

Ross looked disturbed. 'I *have* hurt you. That was the last thing I wanted to do, I've really tried not to let you guess.'

'That was foolish. What sort of marriage would it have been? Hell for both of us. This way we part friends and one day we'll both be glad we came to our senses in time.'

He still held her hand. He look down at it and

only then did she realise it was the hand that bore his ring.

'Keep that, please, will you?' he said and she shook her head, horrified.

'Oh, no I couldn't—it's far too valuable, but I won't give it back here, we don't want people staring.'

'No, we don't,' he said, his eyes flicking briefly across the room and back to her again. He let go of her hand and leaned back in his chair, sighing heavily.

'My God, I feel tired. This sort of scene uses up more energy than a day on the Bahrain site. Melanie, Melanie, will you hit me if I say thank you?' His eyes held a wry smile.

'For letting you off the hook?' she teased. 'It's a relief, isn't it? Like letting go of a heavy weight.'

'For you, too?' He seemed tentative, surprised. They were actually talking to each other openly and easily without any more hesitation or wariness.

'I feel pounds lighter,' she said, laughing.

The waiter appeared and asked if they would like dessert but neither of them wanted anything else to eat. They had coffee and sat smiling at each other like happy idiots because there was no longer any need to watch every word they said; they could just be themselves at last and Melanie felt quite euphoric.

She hadn't breathed a word to Ross about Liz, hadn't asked him any questions or made any hints. Ross was entitled to his privacy. She wouldn't want to talk about Jamie Knox; not, of course, that she was emotionally involved with him, unless you counted wanting to hit him next time she saw him. She distrusted and disliked him but she would not want Ross to know just how passionate her dislike was, or Jamie, either, come to that. He might misinterpret it.

Jamie Knox was an easy man to hate. On that, she and Ross would be agreed, but she kept her silence.

When they got up to leave Jamie and Liz were at the coffee and brandy stage. Melanie fixed a billiant smile and waved to them from the door. They waved back, smiling too. She hoped Liz knew what she was doing. Playing with fire was a lethal game and Jamie Knox was a dangerous playmate. The minute the door had closed on her, she felt her smile wither and bitter aching start up inside her.

Ross gave her an anxious look as he slid her into the front seat of the Rolls. 'Are you okay?'

'Fine,' she said hurriedly. She was just fine—but breaking an engagement had its melancholy side even when it was an amicable arrangement, and she felt bleak and lonely as they drove back.

CHAPTER EIGHT

MELANIE was in bed but wide awake when Liz got home. Lying in the darkness, her mind frantically busy, Melanie heard Liz pause by her door and hurriedly shut her eyes in case her cousin looked into the room. She couldn't face talking to Liz at that moment. After a second or two, Liz tiptoed away and Melanie leaned on her elbow to look at the clock beside her bed. It was gone midnight. They couldn't have been in the restaurant until that hour! Where *had* they been?

She was in a strange frame of mind herself; see-sawing between relief at having escaped from a marriage she had increasingly come to see as a potential disaster, and restless anguish over Jamie Knox.

He had consistently lied to her, by omission, right from the moment they met—what she guessed of his reasons made her bitterly angry and unhappy. He had been using her to get at Ross, hadn't he? Was that what he was doing with Liz now? Had he, too, guessed that Ross was attracted to Liz and far more serious about her than he had been about Melanie?

She should have picked up the vibrations between Ross and her cousin far earlier, but it hadn't even entered her head until Liz gave her that first clue by telling her how Ross had behaved at his secretary's party. Her unconscious had picked up some of the things Liz wasn't telling her, but she hadn't realised that for a time. It wasn't until she heard Liz and Ross speak to each other in that stiff, tense way that the truth clicked inside her head, and the whole picture flashed into focus.

Turning over, she shut her eyes tight, trying to get to sleep, but her mind wouldn't co-operate, it couldn't let go of consciousness. It had too much to process, to work out. It had been an eventful day, but then ever since she met Jamie Knox every day had been an eventful day. He was a catalyst; he caused crisis everywhere he went. What Ross had told her about him hadn't surprised her, once she thought about it. She could imagine Jamie Knox forcing his views on the board of directors, hammering away at them to get his own way, and she could imagine how furious Ross had been. He was possessive about his company; far more passionate about that than he had ever been about her. Jamie couldn't have hit him harder any other way—but had he been trying? Flirting with her, dating Liz—in his own way, Jamie was every bit as ruthless as Ross.

Thinking back over everything Jamie had said to her, she saw that he had been trying to turn her against Ross. He had wanted to see her engagement broken off.

She pushed her palms into her eyes to ease the ache behind them. She wouldn't think about him; he was beneath contempt. What sort of man would set out to wreck someone's life like that? His baffling behaviour was so much clearer, now. First chasing her, then Liz—oh, yes, she understood him now.

What had he said about Liz? 'She was going quietly crazy, she had to talk to someone . . .'

Liz had opened out to him because she needed to talk and Jamie had been only too happy to listen—Liz couldn't have guessed how happy! She had been handing him a weapon to use on Ross. Bitterness twisted Melanie's mouth. No doubt Jamie had been surprised when he met her and heard that Ross was going to marry her. She wasn't the type of woman he would have expected Ross to choose, and he had been right. Ross had for once made a mistake, moved too fast, leapt before he looked, and soon regretted it. Jamie had taken one look at Melanie and must have know that she was out of Ross's league, their relationship would never last. He hadn't been content to watch it founder; he had wanted to cause the wreck himself.

Then Liz had confided in him—and he had realised at once that she was far more Ross's type. Melanie had always been subconsciously aware of that, herself; her cousin's coolness towards Ross had puzzled her from the start. If she hadn't been blinded by her own feelings for Ross she would have paired them off in her mind. Once the first clue got to her, she had rapidly seen the truth.

Jamie Knox had caught on faster than she had, of course. She lay in the darkness, brooding on the tortuous complexity of that mind of his. He was clever, she had to give him that—but he had no scruples. He might be taking an interest in Liz now that he realised Ross was attracted to her, but he hadn't given up with Melanie. That might have puzzled her if she hadn't guessed that he was still applying his brand of pressure in the hope of getting her to break off her engagement.

He wanted to do Ross as much damage as he could, and he didn't care how he did it. Once he knew she had broken with Ross, he wouldn't bother with her any more.

Behind her closed lids danced a flickering series of pictures from earlier that evening—Liz and

Jamie drinking champagne, smiling at each other, talking intimately. How much of that had been acting—how much had been real? Was Liz more *his* type, too? It was probable, she thought grimly. Ross and Jamie Knox were hardly similar, yet they were both sophisticated and intelligent. Jamie might be using Liz, yet he might still enjoy being with her too.

How did Liz feel about him? Melanie's head was beginning to ache. She massaged it crossly with impatient fingers. She didn't find it hard to believe that Liz might fancy Jamie; he had the sort of instant sex appeal which was hard to define but even harder to resist. Melanie felt bleak as she remembered the way they had smiled at each other. It had all seemed so simple when she suddenly guessed that Ross and Liz were attracted to each other. In a flash she had imagined herself solving their problems by giving Ross his ring back, setting him free to go to Liz.

Like all simple plans, it was too good to be true. Ross was free but how did Liz really feel? Melanie had always been fond of her cousin, but she couldn't claim to have understood Liz or known much of what was going on in her head. Liz kept her secrets too well; she wasn't given to indiscretions.

If Liz and Jamie *had* begun an affair, that would complete Jamie's revenge plan, though, wouldn't it? He would have had a part in ending Ross's engagement and he would at the same time walk off with the girl Ross really wanted.

'Damn him,' Melanie whispered to the ceiling. She wished she could think of some equally cunning way of undermining Jamie Knox, but her mind wasn't as complex, she didn't have the Borgia touch he had. She might want to hit back at him, but she would never be able to go through with it.

It wasn't until she was drifting off to sleep that she realised that she had forgotten to give Ross his ring back, after all. She thought hazily about posting it to him, but it was so valuable—what if it got lost in the post? No, she must hang on to it until she saw him again, but first she must break the news to the family. Aunt Dolly was going to be very aggrieved; she had been eagerly looking forward to Melanie's wedding day.

Aunt Dolly and Uncle Teddy got back late on Sunday afternoon. They walked into a spotless house. Melanie had spent most of the morning in an orgy of spring-cleaning which made sure that there was no trace of the party left. She waited until her aunt and uncle had had a cup of tea before she broke the news about the gratecrashers and the broken window.

Aunt Dolly made choking noises, putting down her cup.

Uncle Teddy said: 'They did *what*?' but didn't wait for an answer. 'Did you call the police? Vandals, that's what they are, vandals. Did the police catch any of them?'

'We've had the window replaced,' Melanie said placatingly. 'But the police didn't catch anybody, I'm afraid.'

Her uncle stamped off to view the scene of the crime for himself, muttering ferociously. Aunt Dolly half rose to go too, but sank back.

'Never again. No more parties. I knew something would go wrong, it always does. Where's Will? Taken himself out of the way, I suppose? Afraid to face us?'

Melanie gave her a weak smile; Aunt Dolly

knew her son. Will had gone off on his motor-bike early that morning.

'Where's Liz?' Aunt Dolly asked and Melanie looked away, afraid for some reason of what her eyes might betray.

'She's out, too.' Liz had gone before Melanie came down—Will said Jamie Knox had come for her in his fast red sports-car.

Uncle Teddy came down, grim-faced. 'It was a mistake to go away and leave them to it,' he said. 'Never again.' His wife nodded, her lips tight, in total agreement with him.

Melanie saw that in their over-excited state it would be a serious error of judgment to tell them her other startling news. Aunt Dolly had had enough shocks for one day. The revelation that Melanie's engagement was over would have to wait until tomorrow night when they would have had a chance to get over the story of Will's party.

'Where's Liz?' asked Aunt Dolly again later, and Melanie said that she didn't know. She decided not to mention Jamie Knox; she wasn't sure she could talk about him without sounding bitter.

'Is she playing chicken, too?' Uncle Teddy asked wryly. 'Did they leave you to break the news, Melanie? Isn't that just like them?'

Melanie didn't tell them that Liz had other things on her mind and had probably forgotten all about her brother's party. They would soon find out. It looked as if Jamie Knox was going to become a semi-permanent landmark in their lives.

She went to bed early that evening. Liz and Will hadn't come home. When Melanie came down to breakfast next day she found her aunt and uncle giving Will a bad time. He was sulkily eating cornflakes and trying not to listen, a difficult feat when Aunt Dolly was in such operatic voice. She had a lot to say on the subject of parties, drinking, window-breaking, fighting and anything else that occurred to her and was on her banned list.

Will was glad to get to work, and bolted as soon as he had finished eating, leaving his mother triumphantly in possession of the field.

Melanie had a tiring and difficult day in the office. She had a pile of typing to get through and the phone kept ringing; clients came in a steady stream, wanting details of houses up for sale or asking her to send someone out to give them an estimate for their own home, and she seemed to be running from the moment she arrived at work until the stroke of five-thirty when she could at last shut the front office. George Ramsden and his son were back from a lengthy inspection of an estate possibly coming up for auction by the time she was putting on her jacket to go home.

'I've left some notes on your desk, Mr Ramsden. I think Mrs Silvester has definitely decided to buy the Market Square property. I said you'd ring her. There were quite a few calls and several new clients with houses to sell, but I've left a list.'

Mr Ramsden patted her shoulder. 'Thanks, Melanie. Off you go and you can take the morning off tomorrow. Andrew and I will be here all day, and I owe you some time off.' He preferred to give her the occasional morning off rather than pay her overtime. Melanie smiled wryly, nodding.

'Thank you.' Ever since she had locked the outer door she had been working intensely to finish the typing she hadn't done during the day. It was now six-thirty and she had been at work since a quarter to nine. Sometimes she thought she had picked the wrong job, but on the other hand Mr Ramsden was a kind and likeable man, even if he expected you to work very long hours. At least she had a job, she thought, walking towards her parked car. These days that wasn't something you took for granted.

She unlocked her car and got behind the wheel, her shoulders wearily slumped. A bath, a hot meal and bed were high on her agenda for the evening. She switched on the ignition and frowned. There wasn't a flicker from the engine. She tried again; still nothing.

It was five minutes before she admitted that her car was as dead as a doornail. She got out again, slamming the door. At this hour there was no point in ringing the garage—they would have gone home long ago. She would have to leave her car here and get a taxi home.

As she locked the car door she heard the soft purr of an engine and glanced sideways. A red sports-car was slowing beside her.

Jamie leaned out, raising one brow. 'Having trouble?'

Melanie was tempted to ignore him but it seemed childish so she said curtly, 'My car won't start.'

He drew in to the kerb and braked, getting out, long legs followed by a muscled body and windblown black hair. She felt a tremor of resentment at his height; he dwarfed her. If she ever did try to hit him she would have to aim for his knees.

'Shall I have a look?'

It was a frail hope but she was so tired, she couldn't be bothered to turn down any offer of help, even from a man she loathed and detested. Saving her face seemed, at that instant, less essential than saving her energy.

She slid back behind the wheel, grateful for the chance to sit down, while Jamie vanished under the car bonnet, poking and prying into the engine entrails. Melanie didn't have much hope that he would get it started but he seemed confident that he knew what he was doing. He was an engineer, she thought, presumably he understood engines of most kinds. All the same, she wasn't surprised when he re-appeared with a faint smear of oil across his cheek, slammed down the car bonnet and came to her window, shaking his head.

'Not a chance of starting her, I'm afraid. You'll have to have it towed away in the morning.' He opened the door, standing back. 'Come on, I'll drive you home.'

Melanie got out wearily, re-locked the door and gave him a stiff smile. 'Thank you, but I'll take a taxi.'

She began to walk away; he caught her arm. 'Don't be absurd. Why waste money on a taxi?'

Melanie's temper flared out of control. 'Because I'd rather waste money than have you drive me home!' She wrenched herself away and began walking again, half expecting him to follow her and mentally preparing her iciest brush-off if he did.

She heard his car burst into life but he didn't drive away; he kerb-crawled, leaning out.

'Get in, Melanie.'

She averted her face, quickening her pace. He cruised along beside her, talking. 'Stop making a fool of yourself. This is ridiculous, get in!'

'I don't want to talk to you, go away,' she said, reaching the corner where she hoped to get a taxi.

What she had not anticipated was an interested audience of teenage boys in jeans and bomber jackets, standing outside a nearby café, smoking and idly watching life go by. They all stared at Melanie and her pursuing red sports-car. Their wolf whistles and catcalls made her face burn, she couldn't just stand there under that barrage, so she crossed the road to get away and Jamie did a U-turn in the road, slewing to a sudden stop in front of her before she got to the other kerb.

Melanie gave up. He leaned over and opened the passenger door and she got into the car, ignoring the crude comments from the other side of the road. Jamie accelerated away a second later.

'We made their day,' he said drily.

'You did, you mean! Why did you follow me like that?' She was quivering with temper.

'I've been waiting for you,' he drawled and she did a double-take, staring incredulously at him.

'Waiting for me?'

'For over an hour,' he expanded. 'You work long hours—I hope they pay you well.'

'Why?' she asked huskily.

'If you work this hard you deserve to be paid well,' he returned, but she knew he had understood what she meant because his hard mouth betrayed amusement.

'Oh, stop playing games!' she muttered.

'I haven't started yet,' Jamie mocked.

She counted to ten before she answered that time. 'Why were you waiting for me?'

He halted at traffic lights and put his car into neutral before reaching across her to pick up her left hand. Startled, she watched him stare at the glitter of Ross's engagement ring.

'So you're still wearing it!' He dropped her hand, his face hostile.

'That's right, I am,' she said resentfully. She didn't see why she should tell him that she had, in fact, broken off her engagement. That was what he wanted to hear, of course, but he wasn't hearing it from her. He would find out sooner or later, he could do his gloating then, and with any luck she wouldn't have to watch him do it.

'After what Liz told you?' he asked contemptuously.

'What right do you think you have to discuss my private life with Liz?' she burst out angrily. 'Or with me, come to that? I don't want to talk about Ross.'

'You prefer to shut your eyes to the sort of guy he is, and cling to the thought of all that lovely money, do you?'

She took a sharp, painful breath, turning pale at the insult. She couldn't sit in this car to listen to this—she fumbled with the door handle, intending to get out, but the light turned green at that second and Jamie put on a burst of speed as he moved off, giving her a derisive look.

'You're not getting away from me until you've heard what I have to say!'

She sank back into her seat, fighting to hold on to her temper.

'Did you even talk to him about it?' Jamie asked.

She wouldn't answer; she threw back a question of her own. 'Was it mere coincidence that you and Liz turned up at that restaurant the other day?'

'No,' he admitted calmly. 'I knew it was one of his favourite haunts, that's why I picked it.' He gave her a wry look. 'And it wasn't a coincidence that your car didn't start just now, either.'

Melanie's mouth rounded in a gasp. 'You . . .?'

'Fixed it,' he said with apparent complacency. 'I wanted to talk to you and I had a strong feeling I wouldn't get anywhere if I rang you and asked you out.'

'You put my car out of action?' It hadn't even entered her head that that might explain his sudden appearance at such an opportune moment. Surprise gave way to anger. 'It would serve you right if I rang the police, and I may well do it, too,' she said furiously. 'Who do you think you are? Meddling with everything like that ... following me and Ross about, flirting with Liz, spiking my car ... no wonder Ross sacked you, you must have been a thorn in everybody's flesh.' That reminded her and, working herself up into a towering rage, she demanded, 'And why didn't you tell me that you used to work for Ross and that he'd fired you?'

His dark eyes flicked sideways. 'I didn't want to confuse the issue.'

'You mean that you didn't want me to know that you had a grudge against Ross!'

'It did occur to me that you might misinterpret the news,' he admitted coolly.

'Oh, I haven't misinterpreted it,' Melanie snapped. 'I get the picture only too clearly—you've been trying to use me to get back at Ross. That's why you're so eager for me to break off my engagement. You don't care what you have to do, or how low you have to stoop, so long as you get your revenge! All those cheap gibes about me ... implying that I'm mercenary and that the only reason I got engaged to Ross was because of his money!'

Jamie braked suddenly and she almost went through the windscreen, her body flung forwards violently.

Turning towards her, he asked harshly, 'Are you in love with him? Are you? Be honest, Melanie— look me in the eye and tell me you're in love with him and I'll shut up and go away.'

CHAPTER NINE

MELANIE was filled with a sense of angry hurt. There hadn't been so much as a flicker of regret or apology in his face. He had simply brushed aside her accusations without even trying to deny them. He didn't care what she thought. All he wanted—all he had ever wanted—was to come between her and Ross. That was all she had meant to him from the day they first met—a weapon to use in his war against the man who had sacked him.

'I . . . I'm not g-going to tell you anything,' she said, stammering in helpless rage, her face white and tense. 'I don't want to talk to you. Take me home.'

'Not until you've faced up to the truth,' he said grimly.

'Then I'll walk!'

She swivelled to get out of the car; he caught her shoulder in a grip that made her flinch and flung her round to face him again, leaning over her with those hard dark eyes fixed on her in a hostile stare.

'You're making a bad mistake, Melanie. This dream world you've built for yourself is going to crumble one day, and when it does you're going to find yourself trapped in a painful mess.'

'That's my affair, not yours!'

'He's no more in love with you than you are with him,' Jamie went on brusquely.

'Oh, why won't you shut up?' she wailed like a

142

child, but the emotions she felt were far from childhood, far from anything she had ever known before—a painful mixture of feelings which like some roughly shaken cocktail seemed to be exploding in her body. How was it possible to dislike someone and feel an intense physical attraction all at once? Close to him in the car, she felt her senses work violently. Her cooler mind couldn't stop the process.

'You know I'm telling the truth,' Jamie said, his mouth twisting. 'That's why you're so desperate to stop me.'

'Let me go, you're hurting me!' she said, trying to break his hold.

'At least that's a genuine feeling,' he said. 'If I'm hurting you, and you can feel it, that should tell you something about the way you really feel about Ross Ellis. You're alive now; you know I'm holding you. When you're with him you look like someone sleep-walking, and I'm afraid you're going to sleep-walk into marriage with him and right over a precipice.'

Trembling, she said, 'Ross and I understand each other—we don't need you to act as go-between.'

'Don't be such an obstinate little fool,' he broke out, shaking her. 'I want . . .'

'I know what you want!' she interrupted angrily, and then there was a charged silence while they stared at each other, and Melanie began to feel a peculiar languor; her throat seemed hot and dry, she couldn't breathe properly.

'Do you?' Jamie asked softly, holding her eyes. His head swooped, caught her mouth, the pressure sending her head back against the seat of his car. Melanie fought against a dizziness which made her want to shut her eyes; the feel of his mouth had a sensual warmth that sent slow waves of pleasure through her body. She couldn't think clearly, couldn't keep her mouth closed in spite of her struggle to do so, and her lips parted, yielding and heated.

Jamie wasn't holding her shoulders any more. His hands had travelled, begun exploring; she felt them moving over her body and a harsh groan broke from her. She tried to shake her head, push him away, but his mouth insisted and with that provocative invitation constantly tempting her, her struggles died away and Jamie took her wrists and placed her arms around his neck.

'Kiss me,' he whispered, his lips moving on hers.

Her mind drowned; her body consented, their mouths clinging and the tremors of wild need making her shake from head to foot. Ross had never kissed her like that, never aroused the dormant instincts she was only just discovering existed deep inside her.

Jamie lifted his head a few moments later, breathing thickly. Melanie's fingers were in his thick black hair, her bruised mouth aching as his lips left it, her body quivering passionately, arched against him.

Drowsily, her lids quivered, lifted, the dark blue eyes looked at him in glazed confusion.

'Now tell me you've ever kissed him like that,' he said, staring at her without a smile, and the words were like a slap in the face.

There had been something dreamlike about the caresses they had just exchanged; she had let herself slip helplessly into a fantasy and the awakening was painful. Her face burned in shame and realisation.

She couldn't get out a syllable; her throat was clogged with the dryness of ashes.

'That's why you've got to break off your

engagement,' Jamie said harshly, watching her like an enemy. 'You couldn't kiss me like that if you loved him any more than he would have tried to kiss Liz if he had been in love with you.'

He had been proving his point in a brutal fashion. What did he care if he left her feeling shame and self-contempt?

She sat up, tidying her ruffled hair with shaking hands, turning her flushed face away, hiding the brightness of tears welling up behind her lids.

'Take me home,' she said hoarsely.

Staring intently, Jamie made a rough sound of disgust. 'You mean you still refuse to face the truth? What does it take to get through to you? Don't you understand . . .'

'I understand that you hate Ross and you're trying to use me to get back at him, but it won't work. I'm not being used as a weapon. Just stay away from me in future. I never want to see you again. I don't like you and I don't trust you, so stay out of my life.' Her voice had risen with each word; high and shaky, it was close to tears. With a wild gasp she threw the last words at him, 'Take me home, for God's sake!'

He swung round in his seat, started the ignition and shot away; his profile had frozen into glowering silence. Sitting next to him was like sitting under the very core of a thunderstorm before it breaks—there was no lightning flash, no crash of thunder, but darkness and threat concentrated far too close at hand.

He pulled up outside her home and she stumbled out of the car without saying a word. Jamie only waited for her to slam the door; the next minute he was racing away with a roar of exhaust.

Melanie walked slowly into the house and heard her aunt and Liz talking in the kitchen. She didn't go in to see them, she went straight up to her room and shut the door on herself quickly before anyone could see her face. She stood listening to the over-rapid thudding of her heart, shivering as if in an icy wind. Jamie had proved his point, even if she hadn't admitted it to him, and she was bleakly facing up to the truth, even if it wasn't the truth he had wanted her to face. She was in love with him; she must have been falling in love ever since she first met him. She hadn't wanted to admit it, but just now, in his arms, her reluctant mind had finally caught up with her senses.

It was chemistry, she told herself angrily. That was all it was: mere chemistry. She didn't like Jamie Knox, he was unscrupulous, prepared to use people—the way she responded to him had nothing to do with real love.

'Melanie?' The tap on her door made her jump. She hurriedly dragged a smile into her face before answering Liz.

'Yes?' She wished she could confide in Liz, but she knew she couldn't. She had to lock it all away, never tell anyone. She could only cope with it if she pretended it hadn't happened. After all, it might be another stupid mistake, she might fall out of love as suddenly as she had fallen into it.

'Can I come in?' Liz asked.

'Of course,' Melanie said, hurriedly looking in the mirror and appalled by her own reflection. She was so flushed; she looked hectic. She smoothed down her ruffled hair, and saw the gleam of Ross's ring on her hand. Taking it off she laid it on the dressing-table.

The door opened, Liz came in, smiling. 'Why didn't you come and say you were home? I thought I heard you running upstairs.' Her eyes widened as she saw the discarded ring.

'I'm just coming down,' Melanie said, moving towards the door.

'You've left your ring on the dressing-table.'

Melanie met her cousin's eyes. 'I know.'

Liz turned pale, her lips parting but no sound emerging.

'The engagement's off,' Melanie said.

'Oh, no,' Liz said on a gasp. 'Melanie, you didn't break it off because of what I told you? I'll hate myself. You've got to forget what I said; it didn't mean anything, he didn't do it again. He was drunk.'

'I'm glad you told me. It made it all much easier.' Melanie saw that her cousin wasn't convinced by that. Liz looked almost anguished, her eyes guilty and distressed. Smiling at her, Melanie said, 'You don't understand—Ross and I talked frankly, for the first time and we both admitted we weren't in love, it had all been a mistake.'

Liz looked bleakly at her, wincing. 'Did he tell you that? That he didn't love you? Oh, God, Melly, I'm so sorry, I blame myself . . .'

'You aren't listening properly,' Melanie said, smiling at her. 'I don't love him, either, Liz, and stop looking at me in that guilty way. You did me a favour, honestly. If it wasn't for you I might have married him. I wasn't in love with him at all.'

'You must have been when you got engaged!' Liz sounded incredulous.

'He turned my head,' Melanie said wryly. 'I'd never met anyone like him; he's glamorous and sophisticated and I felt like Cinderella, but it was all a fantasy—a fairy tale. I didn't really know Ross. Jamie Knox said something to me that put it in a nutshell—he said I was sleep-walking, and that's exactly what I was doing. I was going around with my eyes wide open, but I was dreaming. Now I've woken up, and I can see what a mistake I would have made.'

Liz sat down abruptly on the chair behind her. 'You sound very sure,' she said slowly.

'I am,' Melanie said, curling up on the carpet beside her, knees up and her chin resting on them. 'What you told me about Ross making a pass at you didn't actually start the process in my mind, Liz—it was the flashpoint, if you like. I'd been worried about Ross and myself for ages. I never seemed to get to know him any better. I saw so little of him. He seemed to be reluctant to talk to me. Even when we did go out it was always somewhere public—a restaurant for dinner, the theatre, a cinema. I was slow to work it out, but it dawned on me that Ross was keeping me at a distance.'

Liz still looked worried. 'He hurt you . . .'

'No, Liz, he didn't because he couldn't,' Melanie said firmly. 'I was worried, not hurt. After all, we were supposed to get married soon and I was facing up to the prospect of being tied to a man I hardly knew. How could I be in love with him if I couldn't even guess what he was thinking? I tried to tell him; I wanted to talk it out before he went to Bahrain, but Ross was just as evasive then. Of course, he was worried, too, although I didn't realise it. He knew he'd made a mistake but he was too scared of hurting me to tell me so. It was stupid of him, and if we had got married it would all have been much worse. Sooner or later, we'd have had to face up to it.'

Liz was beginning to relax, her face smoothing out into its usual calm. 'Divorce *is* much messier than a broken engagement,' she said drily.

'And far more expensive,' Melanie agreed, laughing.

Liz sobered a moment later. 'When did you tell Ross?'

'We talked it over frankly at lunch in Kendal on Saturday.'

Liz stared. 'On Saturday? But you didn't give him back his ring?'

'It seemed a little public to do it there and then. I meant to give it back in the car later, but it slipped my mind.'

Liz watched her thoughtfully. 'You both seemed very cheerful. It never entered my head that you were discussing breaking your engagement. Whenever I looked over, you were both smiling.'

'We were euphoric with relief,' Melanie said gaily. 'I'm not sure how Ross felt, but I felt like someone breaking out of prison. Do you realise— marriage is a life-sentence?'

Liz laughed. 'You're sure Ross feels the same? I mean, you did ask if he . . .'

'I asked point-blank—we had both been skirting the issue for too long. Ross isn't in love with me any more than I am with him.' She looked steadily at her cousin. 'Stop worrying. I know what I'm doing.'

Liz sighed. 'Jamie said neither of you was in love!'

Melanie's smile vanished. 'Jamie Knox,' she said through her teeth. 'That's something else I want to talk to you about. Did you know he once worked for Ross, and that Ross fired him?'

Liz nodded. 'Yes, he told me that first evening when he brought you home from Ullswater.'

'Did he? And did he tell you that he hates Ross like poison and is looking for a way of getting back at him?' Melanie was pink with anger at the very thought of Jamie Knox. 'Don't trust him, Liz; he'll use you if he can.'

Liz eyed her thoughtfully. 'You don't like him?'

'Do you?'

They stared at each other, their eyes guarded. Melanie couldn't tell what her cousin was thinking and she tried to keep all expression out of her own face.

Aunt Dolly called from the bottom of the stairs, making them both jump. 'Liz? Melanie? Where are you both? The dinner's on the table—aren't you coming down?'

Liz got up. 'Coming,' she called back, then gave Melanie a crooked little grin. 'She sent me to fetch you; it went right out of my head.'

When they went down, Aunt Dolly gave Liz an impatient look. 'Where on earth did you get to? I sent you to look for Melanie, not sit up there gossiping with her!'

Melanie intervened. 'I was telling Liz something . . .'

'Couldn't it wait? Now, come on, sit down and eat this food before it gets cold!'

Uncle Teddy winked at the two girls behind his wife's back. 'Hurry up before she starts on the speech about slaving over a hot stove,' he advised, and Aunt Dolly turned on him too, her blue eyes indignant.

'When I've cooked food, I want it to be eaten—I don't want it sitting about getting cold.'

'It isn't,' Uncle Teddy said, handing Melanie the tureen of vegetables. 'Sit down, Dolly, and stop getting agitated.'

Aunt Dolly subsided into her chair and Will mumbled something about the fried chicken being delicious and he was starving. His mother told him he was always starving, it simply wasn't fair the way he ate so much without putting on an ounce. Will protested, Uncle Teddy teased him, and in the ensuing family discussion it was some time before Aunt Dolly's normally sharp eyes noticed that Melanie was no longer wearing her ring.

It wasn't until Melanie helped her to collect the plates, in fact, that Aunt Dolly noticed her bare finger and gave a startled gasp.

'Melanie! Your ring!'

Melanie flushed slightly, conscious of the others watching her. Aunt Dolly didn't give her a chance to explain. She said in agitation, 'You haven't lost it? Did you take it off to wash? And it's so valuable . . . you shouldn't be careless about anything so valuable, Melanie. I wouldn't have a night's peace if it was mine, I'd always be scared of losing it.'

'Mum,' Liz said gently and her mother's head turned at the note of Liz's voice. 'Melanie has something to tell you.'

It was far harder than it had been when she amazed them all by breaking the news that she was going to marry Ross Ellis. That had been a moment of sparkle and excitement; a champagne day. Melanie could see now how deluded she had been by the sheer surprise of getting engaged to Ross. She had walked into a fairy tale, now she was walking out again. She felt nothing but relief, but she had a shrewd idea that Aunt Dolly wasn't going to be so happy.

She was quite correct; no sooner had she got the words out than Aunt Dolly dropped the plates she was clutching.

'Not going to marry him? What on earth do you mean, not going to marry him?'

Uncle Teddy watched his niece anxiously. 'If you've quarrelled with Ross, I'm sure that . . .'

'It isn't a quarrel, Uncle Teddy, you don't understand.'

'People don't just break off an engagement out of the blue, pet. Something must have happened.'

'We both realised it was a mistake, we don't want to get married,' she said, smiling at him. 'It isn't a disaster, Uncle. We've come to our senses, not lost them.'

'I'm not surprised,' Will said suddenly. 'I never thought he was Melly's type.'

Aunt Dolly turned on him crossly. 'What would you know about it?'

'Are you sure about this, Melanie?' Uncle Teddy asked, and she nodded.

Will had got a dustpan and brush and was on his knees sweeping up the broken plates. 'There's plenty more fish in the sea,' he said airily. 'You'll soon hook someone else.'

'Will Nesbitt, be quiet!' Aunt Dolly snapped, very flushed. 'What on earth are we going to do about the wedding arrangements? The vicar, the hall we booked . . . thank heavens we hadn't got around to having the dress made. And we'll have to tell the rest of the family, all our friends.'

'If Melanie doesn't love the man, there's no point in crying over spilt milk,' Uncle Teddy said. 'Better to find out before the wedding than afterwards.'

Aunt Dolly looked gloomy. 'I suppose so.'

'Don't worry, Mum, Melanie's not going to stay single for long,' said Will. 'I know plenty of guys who'd jump at a chance to date her.'

'Melanie can do better for herself than date one of the bike freaks you go around with,' said Liz drily.

Her brother bared his teeth at her. 'Just because

you're too old for any of the guys . . .' Liz laughed scornfully.

Aunt Dolly sighed. 'As long as you're happy, Melly, that's all I want. I suppose it wasn't meant to be, I did think he was a little old for you but I like him; Ross is a man I respect. I'm sorry it didn't work out for you two.'

'Pin your hopes on Will,' Liz said teasingly.

'Who'd marry Will?' Aunt Dolly retorted. 'Who in her right mind, that is?'

'You'd be surprised how many girls chase me,' Will said, very offended.

'Surprised?' mocked Liz. 'We'd be amazed!'

'A guy in black leathers, riding a high-powered bike, is a big sex-symbol, you know,' Will snarled, and they all laughed.

'Come and help me serve the rice pudding, sex-symbol,' Aunt Dolly said indulgently, and Will was glad to follow her into the kitchen, away from the teasing of his sister.

The weather descended into rainy autumn the following day. The skies were livid, grey clouds clustered, the leaves blew along the gutters, sodden and decaying. People hurried along the pavements, heads bent. Melanie sat at her desk, watching the rain trickling down the windows, listening to the moan of the wind. The weather matched her mood. She didn't know why she felt so depressed; she told herself it was the rain, but she knew she lied.

She tried to get in touch with Ross to arrange to give him back his ring, but he was away again, on business, and Brenda off-handedly said she had no idea when he would be back. Melanie wondered if he had told his secretary that the engagement was over. Brenda had never liked her, Melanie didn't mention anything personal. She just left a message, asking Ross to ring her.

All the rest of the week was the same—the rain was unceasing, there was a chill in the air, the trees lashed backwards and forwards in the wind. Melanie concentrated on her work, went home and watched TV or read until she went to bed, and got up each day feeling grey and melancholy.

On Sunday, though, the weather changed. Autumn vanished and the air was soft and warm, and the sun shone with a poignant fragility which lit the russet leaves and gave a hazy blue shadow to distance.

Over breakfast, Uncle Teddy said wistfully, 'We may not get another day like this until the spring— why don't we all go to the Lakes for the day? A family outing, like the old days? We haven't all been there for ages.'

Will and Liz agreed that it would be fun and Aunt Dolly started planning a picnic lunch to pack for them all, but Melanie hesitated, afraid of running into Jamie at Ullswater. She glanced at Liz secretly, frowning. Was Liz seeing him? She never mentioned him, but then Liz had always been secretive. Melanie felt a sharp little niggle of pain in her chest and bit her lip. She didn't want to find herself face to face with Jamie; it would hurt too much. She didn't want to have to watch him with Liz; that hurt, too. She wasn't jealous of Liz, she was too fond of her cousin—if Liz was happy she was glad, but it hurt, all the same.

'Do you mind if I don't come? I'm expecting a phone call and I'd rather just have a lazy day at home,' she said.

They tried to talk her into it, but she was gently obstinate and in the end they accepted it and went without her. Melanie felt the silence in the house settle like fine dust on her; her spirits sank. They had all looked so cheerful; she envied them. Would

Liz call on Jamie at his cottage, introduce him to her parents?

How wrong she had been about love, how blind when she thought the glamour and excitement of dating Ross meant that she was in love with him. She had believed that falling in love meant a dazzle of light, a sky full of fireworks, each brighter than the one before. The truth was that love was no fun; it was an ache, a deep throb of need, a longing.

She put her hands over her face, shuddering. All week she had been thinking about Jamie; he was never out of her mind. She must stop thinking about him, or she'd go crazy.

She went into the bathroom and began washing her hair, then wrapped it in a towel, turban-fashion, and sat on the edge of the bath while she painted her toenails a delicate pearly pink. Her concentration on this task was broken by a sound she heard downstairs. She froze, head lifted, listening intently, then became quite sure that her ears weren't playing tricks—there was someone downstairs, moving about very softly and furtively.

CHAPTER TEN

MELANIE crept to the bathroom door and opened it carefully, ready to jump back into the room if anyone was within view. She stood there for a second, listening. Was that a stair creaking? Or just her imagination? Her skin was chilly with nerves; she wasn't really certain she had heard anything. This was an old house, full of strange sounds, especially at night or when you were alone in it and instinctively listening to every tiny noise. When there were other people around, it never occurred to you to notice the creaks and rustles.

A minute later she jumped about ten feet in the air, gasping in shock, as a man in black appeared on the landing.

Melanie was back in the bathroom in a flash, but as she began slamming the door she did a double-take of recognition and pulled the door open again.

'You!'

Jamie Knox considered her drily. 'Sorry, did I startle you?'

She clutched the neck of her dressing-gown with a shaky hand, glaring at him with eyes still dilated from the shock of her first glimpse of him.

'Of course you startled me!' she snapped. 'I thought you were a burglar.' He was wearing black jeans and a black sweater with a smooth-fitting turtle neck. He had walked softly because he was wearing grey soft-soled trainers on his feet; it was surprising that she had heard anything at all.

'Sorry,' he said without any apparent regret and she scowled.

'How did you get in, anyway?'

'Through the kitchen door. You really shouldn't leave doors unlocked,' he said lazily, his eyes half hooded by those heavy lids as he studied her. Melanie felt he took too personal an interest in the way her dressing-gown clung to her warm body. She walked past him, bristling, and went downstairs.

'You had no right to walk in here,' she threw over her shoulder.

'Lucky it was only me,' Jamie said coolly. 'Anyone could have got in.'

'So I see,' she said with hostility, turning to face him at the bottom of the stairs. 'That still doesn't explain why you came in and started prowling about.'

'I rang the doorbell, but there was no response, so I went round the back of the house to see if you were in the garden.' He seemed quite unabashed, which made Melanie angrier.

'It would serve you right if I'd called the police when I heard odd noises downstairs!'

He grinned. 'Perhaps it will teach you to take more care in future.'

Her hands clenched at her sides. She felt like hitting him, but he made her too nervous to risk it.

'If you were looking for Liz, she's out,' she told him curtly.

His brows rose. 'All day?'

'Yes, all day.' Melanie felt a roughness in her throat as she watched him. She wasn't jealous, she told herself, she wasn't going to be jealous of Liz, she wouldn't let herself feel like that. What was she going to do if Liz married him, though? She couldn't bear it if they were living near here, if she had to see them together all the time. She would have to go away. It might be cowardice but how else could you deal with a situation like that?

'I see,' he murmured, and his dark gaze wandered over her from her turbaned head to her bare feet. It made her intensely self-conscious when his gaze lingered on her deep-lapelled dressing-gown. She put a hand up to drag her lapels together, to hide the warm curve of her bare breasts from him, and Jamie's eyes fixed on her fingers.

'You aren't wearing your engagement ring.'

She felt her flush deepening. 'I took it off to have a bath,' she evaded. It was stupid to lie but she resented the satisfaction she had heard in his voice. He wanted her to break her engagement to Ross but he didn't care about her feelings.

She saw his brows lift, his eyes harden. 'Seeing him today?'

'No,' she said, then wished she had told another lie. She ought to make him believe she was still seeing Ross.

'Where have your family gone?'

'Ullswater, to sail,' she said.

'You didn't want to go? I thought you loved sailing.'

'I do, but I felt like a quiet day.' She didn't meet his eyes; she didn't want him to guess that she had been afraid of running into him if she visited Ullswater.

'It's perfect sailing weather—a gentle wind and lots of cool sunshine.' Jamie wandered away down the hall and Melanie followed him, frowning.

'Now where do you think you're going?'

'Why don't we have some coffee? I've had a long drive and I'm dying for some coffee.' He calmly began filling the kettle while she watched him, helpless with fury.

'Make yourself at home, won't you?'

The sarcasm was water off a duck's back. He put the kettle on and began to get out two mugs and a jar of instant coffee powder. It was typical of him to do as he pleased without asking permission. Argument with him would be a waste of time and energy.

He turned his head to grin, sunlight striking off the smooth tan of his skin. She felt her heart thud with a crash that sent her nerves jumping, and her mouth went dry.

'I like this house. I gather your uncle and aunt have lived here since they were married.'

She nodded, sitting down abruptly because her knees were giving under her.

'I like old houses,' Jamie said, spooning coffee into the mugs. 'They have more personality than new ones.'

'Your cottage is old, isn't it?' she managed huskily, watching him switch off the kettle and begin to pour the boiling water into the mugs. His body had a vibrant elegance which riveted her stare. At each movement she saw the muscles in his long back flex and relax under the clinging cashmere sweater. His clothes were always good. How was he managing now that he had lost his job? From what Ross had said, she realised Jamie must have earned a considerable sum. Had he saved a lot of it?

'Yes, it's Georgian—but without the frills of the big Georgian houses. Mine is a workman's cottage, but it was built to last. Very solid walls. Almost no foundations, of course, which has meant that I've had trouble with creeping damp, but I've dealt with that problem.' He began to talk about building techniques with the expertise of someone who had studied them, and she listened as she drank her coffee. 'I once thought of being an architect,' Jamie said. 'I enjoy building things, but my personal bent was more towards larger projects—that's why I became a civil engineer. I enjoy seeing a road run where it never ran before, watching a bridge go up over a river. If the underdeveloped countries are to trade successfully, they need better communication, more roads, more bridges. That's the aspect of my work I enjoy the most.'

'Why did you quarrel with Ross over this contract with a foreign government?'

He studied her coolly, his eyes narrowed. 'I didn't like their politics or their reason for offering us the job. I told Ellis my opinion and he told me to mind my own business—company policy was his province. I didn't agree with him. He might be the boss, but that didn't mean the rest of us had no right to an opinion on how the company was run. So I canvassed the rest of the board openly. Ellis was furious, of course.'

'The contract *was* worth a lot of money,' Melanie said, and he grimaced.

'You think that that's all that matters?'

'I think it could hurt the whole firm if Ross only took work from people he approved of,' she said hesitantly.

Jamie gave her a wry smile. 'Maybe, but a lot of people in the firm agreed with me, including quite a few on the board. I think that that was one reason Ellis dismissed me. He resented the fact that I'd swung a lot of people over to my point of view. He likes to keep the reins firmly in his own hands. He doesn't like interference in his decisions. So I had to go.' His eyes glinted. 'I got quite a handsome settlement—he was afraid I'd sue him and the publicity of the case could harm the firm, so he gave me a golden handshake.'

Her eyes widened. 'Is that why you're in no hurry to find another job?'

'Partly. I've been working very hard for some years, I felt I was entitled to some time off before I started looking for new employment.'

'Won't you find it hard, though? I mean, if Ross gives you a bad reference?'

'I'm pretty well known in my own field. I've already had several approaches, but I'm not ready to make up my mind yet.'

'Would it mean working abroad again?' she asked, finishing her coffee and putting down the mug. If he married Liz, it would make it easier to bear if they lived abroad; Melanie wouldn't have to keep up an act all the time.

'That's the question,' he said, his face wry. 'I wouldn't want to, if it could be avoided. I've had enough wandering. When I was younger I had the travel-bug badly, I couldn't wait to get on a plane for new places. I must be getting old.' He grinned at her. 'How about you? Do you like travelling?'

'Not much,' she admitted. 'I'm happy living here—where else would you find such breathtaking scenery? This part of England is so rich in history, too—Hadrian's Wall, for instance. We used to take a picnic up there in the summertime and walk along the wall until we found somewhere peaceful where we could eat our lunch and look at the view. My father . . .' She broke off, her eyes lowered, and was silent for a second, until she went on huskily, 'He was very interested in Roman history.'

'It must have been a traumatic shock, when he and your mother were killed,' Jamie said gently and she nodded without looking at him. 'Liz said that you were badly injured yourself, in the crash.'

'I was ill for ages. I hated hospital. I've hated

the sight of white coats and the smell of disinfectant ever since.'

There was a silence, then she forced herself to look up and smile brightly.

'I was lucky to have Uncle Teddy and Aunt Dolly there—not to mention Liz and Will.'

'You're very fond of them. You'd miss them if you had to move away, wouldn't you?' Jamie said oddly, and she wondered if he was realising how much she would miss Liz if he married her cousin and took her abroad.

Flatly, she agreed. 'In many ways, they're closer than a real brother and sister. Liz and Will squabble with each other far more than they ever did with me. We're all very close.'

'That must be comforting,' Jamie said gently, watching her with warmth in his dark eyes. She felt a sharp pain inside her chest. He shouldn't smile at her like that; it wasn't fair. It hurt.

She got up suddenly. 'I have a lot to do today, I'm afraid—why don't you go back to Ullswater and find Liz?'

He got to his feet more slowly, his brows dark above his watchful eyes.

'Melanie . . .' he began and she was disturbed by the note in his voice. Turning, she began to hurry towards the door, but his hand caught her shoulder and spun her to face him. The way he looked at her made her pulses go crazy; she almost hated him for making her feel like that. He knew what he was doing; it was intentional, all part of his plan to get his own back on Ross.

'You must go,' she said thickly, shivering.

'You don't want me to go,' Jamie said in a low, deep voice, his other hand caressing her flushed cheek. If she had her eyes closed she would recognise the feel of his fingers on her skin, she thought dazedly, trying to back away from the incitement of that gentle touch.

'How can you?' she asked bitterly, turning her head to avoid his searching mouth. 'No, don't. I don't want you to kiss me.'

'Yes, you do,' he whispered against her cheek, that insistent mouth moving closer while she struggled to break away.

'You came here deliberately,' she accused. 'I wouldn't be surprised to find out that you knew I was alone—did you see Liz and the others at Ullswater? Did you guess I was here by myself?'

'Yes,' he said shamelessly, kissing her neck, and she might have guessed from the start if she hadn't been so taken aback to see him.

'What sort of man are you?' she asked angrily, throwing back her head to look at him with hatred, and that was a mistake because it gave Jamie the chance he had been waiting for.

His mouth hit hers a second later, and temptation caught her by the throat, her own desire overwhelming her common sense. His kiss weakened her resistance; she felt herself kissing him back, her body trembling violently. Chemistry, that's all it is, she told herself, but her senses drowned that cold little voice. She had her eyes shut, her head was thrown back, the towel tumbling off and her damp hair cascading down her back. Jamie pulled her even closer; one hand slid inside her dressing-gown and caressed her bare breasts. Her skin burnt, the intimacy of the touch driving her crazy.

Did it matter why he was making love to her? she thought wildly. What did anything matter, except that she needed to have him kiss her, needed to be in his arms, closer and closer in this drowning sweetness?

A second later the shrill of the telephone made

her jump. Jamie started, too, lifting his head and staring at her with glazed eyes, as if he had been as far away as Melanie while they kissed.

'Ignore it,' he said, as she began to pull free. He tried to kiss her again but she broke away and almost ran to the phone, her legs shaky.

'Hallo?' she asked huskily, holding the receiver in trembling fingers.

'Melanie, is that you?'

'Ross,' she said, shock in her voice and across the hall her eyes met Jamie's. He was scowling, his body tense, his hand raking back his dishevelled hair.

Melanie swallowed in dismay at the folly she had almost committed—Jamie had just been using her, he didn't have any real feeling for her. He just wanted revenge on Ross, and of course it mattered why he had tried to make love to her. She must have been insane even to consider letting him kiss her.

Ross was talking brusquely in her ear; she barely heard what he said. He had got her message but he wouldn't be back for some time. What did she want? Was it urgent?

'It doesn't matter, Ross,' she said. 'I'll see you when you get back, ring me the minute you do.'

She hung up and Jamie came towards her, his face hard. He opened the door without a word. The slam of it made her nerves flicker violently.

She ran upstairs and flung herself on her bed, weeping passionately. It was a long time before she was able to reach some sort of calmness, and it was the stoicism of despair by then. She had to face the fact that she was deeply in love with a man who had no scruples and no heart. For a time today as they talked she had liked him very much, but he had fooled her again. He was so easy to like and so dangerous to trust.

Never again, she thought, as she dressed and blow-dried her hair into shape. She would never let him get to her again.

When she saw Liz later that evening, she discovered that Jamie had gone back to Ullswater and that Liz and Will had had drinks with him at the pub, then the whole family had gone along to meet his parents at their home. Melanie felt a stab of jealousy at this news. He must be serious about Liz, or why would he take her to meet his parents? she thought miserably.

'I liked them,' Liz said. 'His father's a darling— very like Jamie. He was a sailor, did you know? They have a boat, bigger than ours. They seem very happy together. Their house is charming; small but delightfully furnished.'

Melanie forced a smile. 'Is it Georgian, too?'

She half listened as Liz talked about the Knox family, half fought an inner sense of grief because she hadn't met his parents, hadn't seen his home.

Damn Jamie Knox, she thought, how can he live with himself, acting the way he does? Doesn't it occur to him that I might tell Liz about the pass he made at me today? Or is he so sure of her that he thinks he could talk his way out of any accusation? But then he knows us so well now, he probably guesses that I couldn't tell Liz, any more than she wanted to tell me about the night Ross kissed her. I couldn't deliberately hurt Liz, any more than she could deliberately try to hurt me. I'm silenced by my affection for Liz, and Jamie Knox knows it.

'What a pity you weren't with us,' Aunt Dolly said. 'Jamie's parents were so disappointed; they were hoping to meet you.'

Melanie looked at her in disbelief and surprise.

She couldn't believe that Jamie's parents had even heard of her, but then Aunt Dolly's love for them all had always blinded her.

She was glad to get back to work on Monday morning; keeping busy was the best way of keeping her mind off Jamie Knox. As the week went by, she was surprised not to hear from Ross. He seemed to have been away a long time. She rang his office and Brenda was icily off-hand. Ross was still away; no doubt if he wanted to speak to Melanie he would have given her a call. As he hadn't, Brenda could only say that she had passed on Melanie's message, the rest was up to Ross himself. Flushed, Melanie rang off.

The following Friday Melanie was alone in the office when the bell fixed above the street door jangled. Melanie thought that it would be Mr Ramsden back from lunch with his bank manager. She looked up, smiling.

The smile died as she recognised Jamie Knox. She didn't move from her desk, her body rigid as she stared at him with hostility. He let his gaze drift over her, his brows arched as he took in the simple blue sweater, the pleated white skirt and all the other details of her appearance—she was made to feel that he had even noticed that her nose was shiny and her lips had only a faint trace of pale pink lipstick. The way she looked hadn't bothered her until that moment. She was a working girl; not a fashion model.

Now, though, faced with Jamie Knox in a casually elegant dark suit, crisp shirt, silk tie, she ground her teeth impotently under that derisory stare.

He tapped peremptorily on the counter. 'Miss!'

Melanie began to type again, ignoring him.

'Excuse me, miss,' he said, leaning over the

counter, a lock of thick black hair falling over his eyes. He looked like an Old English sheepdog after a heavy night, she though viciously. Aloud, she said, 'Leave me alone and go away.'

'You know you don't want me to do that,' he purred, and she hit the keys with punishing precision. God knows what I'm typing, she thought. I certainly don't, but I will not . . . will not! look at him again.

'I'm interested in a property you're advertising,' he said in a silky tone which made her face hot and her temper flare.

'I'm too busy to deal with you, clear off,' she said furiously.

'Miss Nesbitt!' Mr Ramsden's horrified voice made her go crimson to her hairline. She looked round, dumb with shock. She might have expected him to use the back door after lunch with his bank manager. That always made him feel depressed and furtive. But why did he have to arrive just in time to hear her flinging insults at Jamie Knox?

She hung her head, unable to meet her boss's aghast stare. What on earth could she say in her own defence? It was fate. She was doomed. Every time she set eyes on Jamie Knox she could expect disaster.

'I'll talk to you later,' Mr Ramsden threatened before turning to Jamie Knox, his smile placatory.

'Please accept my apologies—I simply don't know what's wrong with young people today. Unforgivable, quite unforgivable. I can promise you, she won't get away with it.'

Melanie flashed a dart of rage at Jamie Knox through her lowered lashes. His mouth was crooked with triumphant mockery. He thought it was funny, did he? She was tempted to get up and throw her typewriter at him, but she suppressed the impulse. She had enough trouble as it was.

'How can I help you?' asked Mr Ramsden, bending over the counter with a smile. 'Mr . . .?'

Jamie ignored the polite query. 'I'm looking for a four-bedroomed house close to Carlisle; detached, with a good garden and a garage. Have you got anything of the sort on your books?'

Mr Ramsden beamed. Whatever a client wanted, he was always sure he could produce exactly what was required.

'Certainly, certainly. We have a very wide selection of properties and I'm sure we can find you what you're looking for. Please, come into the inner office, Mr . . .?'

Jamie had witheld his name the first time he was asked but now he said, 'Knox. James Knox, Mr Ramsden. It is Mr Ramsden?'

'It is indeed.' Mr Ramsden lifted the counter and Jamie strolled through the gap. He deliberately leaned on Melanie's desk while he observed her rigid countenance. She typed like a thing possessed, her eyes fixed on the paper, refusing to admit she knew he was there although she could see the brown hand out of the corner of her eye; the long fingers splayed on her desk, the crisp white cuff of his shirt half concealing his wiry wrist. An odd little shiver ran down her spine as she looked; a sharp stab of awareness piercing her ribs.

She hurriedly stopped glancing that way, riveting her eyes on what she was typing, but behind her half-lowered lids she still saw his tanned skin, the faint blue of the veins in his wrist, the individual shape of those long, cool fingers. Her mouth was dry; he had touched her with those fingers, her skin burned at the memory.

'This way, Mr Knox,' her boss said, opening the

door into the inner office. 'Please, take a chair, I'll be with you in a minute.' He closed the door and turned round, glaring, hissing at her in a tone calculated not to be heard on the other side of the door, 'Melanie, what on earth possessed you? I'd think you were drunk if I didn't know you better. I can only think you're tired. Maybe I've been over-working you. I'll be charitable and say that that explains it, but if it ever happens again . . .'

'It won't,' she said hurriedly, very pink. 'I'm sorry, Mr Ramsden, but I thought he was just a time-waster, I didn't believe he really wanted to buy a house here.'

Mr Ramsden frowned. 'Why on earth should you think that? Has he been in before? I don't remember the name.'

'No, I . . . he . . . it was a mistake,' she said, flustered. 'I'm sorry, mistaken identity, I thought he was someone else.'

Mr Ramsden considered her soberly. 'All the same, even if he had been a time-waster you shouldn't have spoken to him like that. How many times do I have to tell you? However much of a nuisance someone is, be polite at all times, even if you feel like throwing something at him.'

'Yes, Mr Ramsden,' she said with meek eyes lowered. 'I'm sorry.'

'So I should think. We might have lost a valuable client. Now, look out all the details of suitable houses for me and bring them in to us in a minute. I'll give him a drink and fill out the form in the meantime.' Mr Ramsden looked at his watch. 'I've got an appointment at four-thirty, so there won't be time for me to show him any houses today, but he can study the details of anything you find in the files and I'll make appointments for him to view those he wants to see. Tomorrow will do, I don't suppose he's in a tearing hurry.'

He went into the other room, and Melanie began pulling out details of every detached or four-bedroomed house they had on their books. As always, she included several houses which fitted neither description. People were so unpredictable; they came in with a list of requirements, then chose something completely different, which had taken their fancy.

Was Jamie serious about wanting to buy a house? Or was he playing one of his games? He had seemed so happy with his little cottage on Ullswater—why should he want to buy a large house near Carlisle?

Unless, she thought, pausing with a bleak look on her face, unless he was thinking of getting married?

She bit her lip, then angrily gathered up all the sheets she had pulled from the filing cabinet and took them into the other office. Jamie sat on the other side of Mr Ramsden's desk, lounging in a negligent pose, his jacket unbuttoned and a glass of whisky in his hand. His black hair gleamed in sunlight and he followed Melanie's movements out of the corner of his eye as she walked over to the desk.

She refused to look at him. It was inexplicable how she managed to notice so much, all the same. He had crossed his legs, one polished shoe swung idly. She kept her eyes down as she placed the pages on the blotter in front of Mr Ramsden and withdrew at his nod.

She got on with her work, trying not to catch the deep calm tones of Jamie's voice in the other room. It must have been half an hour later when the door opened and Mr Ramsden re-appeared, looking harassed.

'Melanie, Mr Knox insists on viewing Steynsforth House this afternoon,' he said grimly. 'Apparently his time is limited and he's in a rush to find a house.' He gave her a shrug. 'You were way off course about the time-wasting; that is a man in a hurry and he certainly doesn't mean to let the grass grow under his feet. I can't take him there, I've got more urgent business as I told you—you'll have to show him round.'

Melanie's heart plummeted. 'Me? I can't.' She caught Mr Ramsden's impatient eyes and stammered, 'I'm not very good at taking people round the houses, you know that. Why can't the owners show him round?'

'Because the house is empty,' Mr Ramsden snapped. 'Old Aggie Steynsforth died a year ago, the house is only just out of probate and the new owner lives in Spain and doesn't want to waste any more time selling the house. If we can sell it to this client I'll be very relieved. The owner promised me a bonus if the house was sold within the next month and I never thought I'd collect it. It's in bad need of repair and the garden's a jungle. But try to talk him into it.' He bent a stern eye on her. 'And be very, very polite. Do you understand, Melanie?'

Melanie nodded, biting her lip. 'Yes, Mr Ramsden.'

'Your job could well depend on it,' he threatened.

'Yes, Mr Ramsden,' she repeated, keeping her smouldering eyes lowered. If Jamie Knox was playing games and had no intention of buying a house she would kill him, but until she was sure what he was up to she could not take the risk of saying or doing anything that Mr Ramsden could disapprove of. Jamie wouldn't hesitate to give her boss a lurid description of her behaviour if she stepped out of line again.

No doubt he was laughing like mad behind that polite smile he wore as he came forward to meet her. He had her trapped; she was going to have to smile at him and talk with honeyed courtesy. That didn't mean she had to like it. Or him.

'We'll take my car,' Jamie said softly, his dark eyes glittering with mockery.

'Certainly, sir,' Melanie said sweetly, collecting her handbag and jacket. Jamie held the door open for her. She briefly raised her eyes to him as she said, 'Thank you, Mr Knox,' in the same saccharine tone. Her stare said something very different; her blue eyes hated him and Jamie Knox laughed. Melanie walked into the street, teeth gritted. How dare he laugh at her?

CHAPTER ELEVEN

SHE sat next to him in the sports-car in offended silence. Jamie didn't appear to notice. He whistled softly as he drove, the wind raking back his hair and his profile amused. Melanie didn't have to give him directions; Mr Ramsden had done that. She had seen Steynsforth House from the outside many times; it was a solid Victorian house set in walled grounds which had become overgrown, so that one caught glimpses of the faded cream of stucco through tangled branches of trees and bushes. The rhododenrons had grown so high and spread so far that they had become a thick hedge.

Jamie parked on the drive and they walked through rustling leaves to the front door. Jamie paused, looking around at the almost bare branches, the tall, leaf-littered lawns which hadn't been mowed for months by the look of them, the grassy paths and weedy flowerbeds.

'Melancholy, isn't it?'

He shrugged as she unlocked the door, without replying. 'How long has it been empty?'

'A year.'

The hall was dusty and gloomy; the light filtering through those thick-set trees had a greenish hue. Melanie felt like someone walking on the bottom of the sea.

'These panels are original,' she said, reading from the sheet of details she had got from the file.

'Oak. The hall is fifteen foot by twelve, a very spacious . . .'

'I know all that, I read it,' Jamie said, taking the sheet from her and pushing it into his pocket.

Melanie bristled. 'Do you want to see the rest of the house? Or have you seen enough?'

'I haven't seen anything yet,' he said, walking past her into a large, square room. The furniture had been sold at auction and had fetched quite a good price because it was largely early nineteenth-century stuff and in good condition. Jamie looked up at the stuccoed ceiling with its swags of flowers and geometric designs, then at the pale blue walls. Every step he took made the bare floorboards creak. The house had that strange echo you always find in empty houses. Bushes tapped at the windows, swaying in the autumn wind. Melanie shivered, aware of the silence and isolation and oppressed by them.

Jamie went out and explored the rest of the ground floor. She followed him at a distance, waiting for him to tire of whatever game he was playing. He couldn't seriously intend to buy this house, not now that he had seen it. There was a faint smell of damp in every room; the floorboards were uneven and, she strongly suspected, might have dry rot. You would have to spend money to make it habitable, and there were far too many rooms for a normal-sized family, let alone a single man.

'This will all have to come out,' he said in the kitchen, wrinkling his nose at the ancient stove, the old-fashioned cupboards and dresser. 'It's quite a sizeable room, though. Polly will like that.'

Melanie's heart stopped. He was opening a cupboard, taking out a tin of mustard that looked as if it had been there since the start of the century.

'Polly?' she asked huskily. He had never mentioned the name before—was this Polly the girl he really intended to marry? Melanie had never liked the name Polly; she imagined this unknown girl with bitter dislike. Beautiful, no doubt. She would be, wouldn't she? If Jamie preferred her to someone as sleekly elegant as Liz, Polly had to be someone very special. Or did she have money? Jamie had seemed so convinced that Melanie only wanted to marry Ross for his money—was that why he was planning to marry this Polly?

'My sister,' he said casually, walking out.

Melanie shut her eyes. She felt faintly sick. His sister! Polly was his sister.

She ran after him. 'Are you looking for a house for your sister?'

'And her husband and three children,' Jamie said, grinning down at her. 'They've been living in Nigeria for four years—David's an architect, he's been working on government projects out there, but his contract is finished and he and Polly are coming home for good, so they want a big house that David can take to pieces and put back together again.' He put a foot on the bottom stair, his hand gripping the carved newel post. 'David plans to work from home in future. He's setting up his own firm and this house has plenty of room for an office. He'll have great fun redesigning it to suit their needs—typical architect, can never leave a house alone.' He gave her a brief look. 'He used to work for Ross Ellis, too.'

Melanie watched him turn away and start to climb the stairs. 'Was he fired, too?'

'No, he quit to take up this job in Nigeria,' Jamie said without looking back. 'He and Ellis got on quite well, actually. David is very easy-going; he did what he was told and never argued. Just the sort of employee Ellis likes.'

'Ross can't be as bad as you pretend—he's built up that firm in a very short time and he employs hundreds of people who wouldn't have a job if it weren't for him!' Flushed, Melanie followed him and he threw her a sardonic look.

'Still defending him? I thought you'd finally seen sense and broken off your engagement.'

She stood completely still on the landing, hearing him walk across a bedroom, his footsteps echoing in the empty house. So he did know. Liz had presumably told him.

He re-appeared and stood looking at her, his hands on his hips and hostility in his dark eyes. 'But perhaps you regret it?' he mocked icily. 'Hankering for all that cosy security, are you?'

'I'm getting sick of listening to remarks like that,' she said angrily. 'I'm not putting up with any more insults from you. I'll wait outside in the car. When you've seen the rest of the house, let me know and I'll come and lock up.'

She turned to go back downstairs, but found him barring her way; a dark impatience in his face.

'Oh, no, you don't, you're not running out this time, you little coward,' he said scathingly.

His eyes glittered in the shadowy light on the landing; his face was all angles, hard and menacing. Melanie swallowed, backing.

'You don't frighten me,' she lied, wishing she would stop trembling. He was so tall and powerful and the house was so empty around them. The sound of their breathing seemed very loud.

'I should frighten you, Melanie,' he said, a leashed violence in his voice. 'I'm going to make you face up to the truth.'

She had backed into one of the bedrooms; all the furniture had gone but the room still held occupants—Melanie's worried eyes caught the scuttle of a spider along a swaying silken thread on the wall.

'I don't know what you're talking about,' she said.

'Don't you?' He took another step and was far too close. 'Oh, I think you do. You knew long ago, and so did I.'

'Knew what?' she whispered, her throat rough.

'This!' he said huskily, a hand curving about her face. She could have pushed him away, he wasn't using force, but she didn't; even though she despised her own weakness. He slowly bent and she watched his mouth with a hunger that shocked her. As it touched her lips she closed her eyes and put her arms round his neck, kissing him back in helpless desire. She was going to hate herself tomorrow, but at that moment it didn't seem to matter. Nothing mattered except the hot exchange of passion; his hand moving down her spine, over her body, his hair running through her trembling fingers.

Jamie whispered something against her mouth, the words so smothered she only realised what she had heard a minute later, and she stiffened in his arms.

'What?' she asked, pulling her head back and staring at him, her dark blue eyes wide and glazed.

He stared into them, his mouth crooked, a flush on his face. 'I love you,' he repeated and she closed her eyes again, shuddering. From behind her lids tears trickled and Jamie's arms tightened.

'Melanie? What is it? Don't. Why are you crying?'

'Nothing,' she said shakily, half laughing.

She opened her eyes again and saw bewilderment and anxiety in his face.

'What do you mean—nothing? People don't cry over nothing,' he said harshly.

She pushed him away, running a hand over her wet eyes. 'You didn't mean it. You're not in love with me. You only want to use me to get back at Ross.'

Jamie stiffened, his face tense. 'What?'

'Did you think I hadn't worked it out? You're wrong. You're a lot more obvious than you think you are.'

'Oh, am I?' he said slowly, watching her intently. 'You thought I was chasing you to annoy Ellis, did you?'

'Well, weren't you?' Her chin went up, she fought not to show how much that hurt her. 'It was Liz you were really interested in . . .'

'Liz?' His brows shot up and he laughed shortly. 'Are you crazy? Liz is head over heels in love with Ellis and has been for months. If you weren't so blind you'd have noticed, long ago.'

Melanie looked at him with contempt. 'Of course, you saw it right away, didn't you?'

'Yes,' he said coolly. 'The first time I met her, we had dinner and talked and something she said suddenly made it very obvious. When I made it clear I'd guessed, she didn't deny it. I think it was relief to be able to talk openly. She'd been hiding it for too long.'

'And I suppose you guessed Ross fancied her, too, after she'd told you about the pass he'd made at her?'

'It occurred to me,' he admitted without shame.

'And so you chased both of us,' Melanie said bitterly. 'You really meant to get Ross, didn't you?'

His dark eyes held violence again. 'I ought to slap you,' he said and she backed.

'You do and I'll . . .'

'What?' he mocked, grabbing her.

This time she fought, her body struggling helplessly in his hands. He held her, watching her with an angry smile, knowing she couldn't match his strength.

'Tell me you love me,' he said in silky provocation.

She bared her teeth, hissing through them, 'No!'

'Never?' he asked, arching his brows.

'Never, never, never,' Melanie yelled, writhing in his grip.

'Not even after we're married?' he enquired lazily and she looked at him in desolation and fury.

'I could kill you! How can you? You're a bastard and I hate you.'

'Liar,' he said, pulling her inexorably towards him, her struggles completely unavailing. Her feet skidded along the bare floorboards and Jamie gave a final jerk which sent her tumbling into his arms, held too tightly to be able to escape. She turned her head from side to side, breathing thickly, but in the end his mouth closed over her lips and a moment later Melanie gave up fighting and kissed him back.

Jamie ran his hand through her ruffled hair, looking down at her flushed face, some time later.

'I love you, Melanie,' he said softly. 'And I mean it. I want to marry you.' His fingers stroked her hot cheek. 'Now, tell me . . .'

Drowsily, she lifted her lids. 'Tell you what?'

His hand closed round her throat. 'Torment.' He kissed her quickly, lightly, lifting his mouth before she could kiss him back. 'Tell me you love me.'

'You're so sure I do,' she said, grabbing a handful of his hair and tugging it. 'What makes you so sure?'

He smiled at her and her heart turned over. 'A look in your eyes.' He brushed a finger over her lids and she shut her eyes. 'The look I saw then,' Jamie said. 'It makes me think you feel the way I do. Am I wrong?'

She leaned her head on his shoulder. 'No,' she whispered. 'I love you.'

His arms held her so tightly that she could scarcely breathe. For what seemed a very long time they didn't speak, leaning against each other, their bodies still and their hearts beating together. Melanie felt a deep peace, that poised calmness which comes before sleep. The confusion, anxiety and misery of the past few weeks fell away and everything dropped into place, she understood at last.

'The first time I saw you,' Jamie murmured conversationally. 'The very first time, I fancied you, even though you were snarling at me like a wildcat because I'd taken your parking space.'

'Taken?' she retorted, lifting her head. 'Stolen, you mean. You knew I was going to back into it! Didn't you?'

He grinned. 'I didn't know whether you were coming out or going in,' he admitted shamelessly. 'But as the space was empty, I went into it. I was in a hurry, I was late meeting someone.'

Melanie remembered the girl he had been with in the bar and frowned. 'Was she someone special?' she asked with pretended indifference, and his eyes teased.

'She thought so.' Then he laughed, shaking his head. 'No, that was our second date and our last. If I hadn't met you, I might have gone on dating her for a while but it wouldn't have come to anything—she was pretty but selfish, a spoilt little rich girl. Her father is one of the directors of Ellis's firm.'

Melanie looked down, sighing at the mention of Ross. 'Oh, look at the time,' she said, catching sight of Jamie's watch as his fingers moved gently against her shoulder. 'Mr Ramsden will wonder what on earth I'm doing.'

'When we tell him we're getting married, he'll know what we were doing,' Jamie said casually, and she went pink.

'No! I couldn't . . .'

Jamie stopped smiling, his face taut and intent. 'What do you mean, you couldn't? I asked you to marry me, Melanie, I thought you . . .'

'I mean I can't tell anyone, not yet, not so soon after breaking off my engagement to Ross; it would make me feel stupid.'

He watched her, those dark eyes hard. 'Stupid to break off your engagement to him—or stupid to get engaged to me instead?' he asked harshly and Melanie looked at him with passionate impatience.

'Oh, don't be so edgy, Jamie. I didn't mean that at all. Don't you see how changeable I'm going to look? People are going to think I can't make up my mind, they'll laugh at me!'

His face relaxed and he grimaced. 'I suppose you have something there, but does it matter what people think? You made a mistake over Ellis. So what? People do, even if they don't like admitting it. None of us is perfect.'

'No, but I rushed into an engagement with Ross and it was a mistake, so I'm afraid to rush into anything any more. We ought to take some time to get to know each other before we make any snap decisions.'

He considered her wryly. 'You've got that obstinate look again. Are you serious?'

She nodded and he shrugged without heat. 'It doesn't mean I'm not sure, Jamie,' she said huskily, stroking his cheek. 'I am. But all the same, I think we ought to take it slowly. I don't want to send Aunt Dolly into hysterics.' She gave him an uncertain glance, biting her lip. 'And then there's Ross . . .'

He stopped smiling, again. 'You do regret giving him up?'

'No,' she insisted. 'But I can't help wondering if you want me simply because you hate Ross so much.' Her dark blue eyes pleaded. 'You've always been so hostile to him, about him. You would like to get back at him, wouldn't you?'

Jamie exploded, scowling at her. 'My God! You still think I'm using you? What do I have to do to convince you? I love you, you stupid woman. I've never said that to any other woman and it wasn't a glib, easy thing to say. I meant every word!'

'I'm sorry, Jamie,' she stammered, terrified by the rage in his voice.

He looked at her, violence in his dark eyes. 'So you damned well should be. You're right, we'd better not talk about marriage yet. Obviously, you don't trust me and that means you can't really care that much for me, either.'

'No,' she said shakily, clinging to him. 'I do, Jamie. I love you but I'm still confused. The way you chased me from the start made me think it was Ross you were really trying to get at, can't you see that?'

He stared into her lifted eyes, still frowning. 'Only a woman would come up with such tortuous thinking. Look, I was furious with Ellis when he fired me, but it was business, not personal. What the hell do you think I am? What makes you imagine that I'd try to use a woman to get my own back on Ellis? Revenge is petty and pointless, anyway. What good would it do me to stab Ellis in the back? If I kept trying to get you to break off your engagement, it was because I was in love with you and I had a strong hunch that it was mutual. Right from the night we spent on the fells I could see that you and Ellis weren't right for each other. I know the man, remember.'

Melanie gave a long, deep sigh of relief. 'I'm sorry, Jamie, I misunderstood.'

He framed her face between his hands, his eyes brooding on her. 'I wish I didn't love you so much.'

Staring into his eyes, she understood him for once and smiled quiveringly. 'I know, I feel the same. That's how I knew I wasn't really in love with Ross. He couldn't hurt me, the way you can.' She stared at his mouth, her throat hot. 'But then he never got to me the way you do.'

Jamie kissed her fiercely and she wound her arms around him, kissing him back with all the intense feeling inside her.

They drove back to the office ten minutes later and found Andrew coping with the late afternoon rush. While they were talking to him about the Steynsforth house Mr Ramsden came back and beamed with delight to hear that he had probably sold the old house.

'I'll put down a deposit on it now and then my sister should be here next week to confirm the sale. I'm sure the house is just what they're looking for—in the meantime, I'll get a surveyor to look at the place and give me a report on it.' Jamie followed Mr Ramsden into the inner office to discuss the details and Melanie went back to her desk, but it was impossible to work with any real concentration. Her mind kept wandering and she was absent-minded, she kept making mistakes in her typing.

By the time Jamie and Mr Ramsden emerged from the other room, it was five-thirty and Melanie was putting the cover on her typewriter. Jamie shook hands with Mr Ramsden, smiling at him. 'I'll be in touch, then. Goodnight.'

He walked out of the door and Mr Ramsden spoke to his son about another matter, giving Melanie a vague glance as she put on her jacket and collected her bag.

'Good work, Melanie. We're going to get that bonus on the Steynsforth place after all. You see, you never know what you're going to be able to sell in this business. That's what I love about it.'

She smiled, saying goodnight to both him and Andrew, and left. There was no sign of Jamie but as she reached her parked car, she saw his car purring towards her. He leaned out, his eyes gleaming wickedly.

'Want a lift, lady?'

Laughing, she got into the passenger seat. 'Mr Ramsden is going to think my car has broken down again!'

Jamie drove off with a surge of power from the sports-car's engine. 'That old thing is ready for the scrap-heap, anyway.'

'Do you mind?' she retorted defiantly. 'I love my car, even if it is old.'

'It belongs in a car museum. I'm amazed it goes at all.'

'Well, it was all I could afford,' she said, smiling at him.

'Which reminds me, I've got an interview with a big engineering firm on Tuesday,' Jamie said. 'Most of their work is done in the UK so I won't have to be abroad all the time, the way I was with Ellis.' He grinned sideways at her. 'Keep your fingers crossed that I get the job.'

She let her head slide on to his shoulder, smiling. 'They are crossed,' she murmured, showing him.

He turned into the road in which she lived and drew up outside her home, behind another car which they both recognised.

Jamie stared at it. 'What's Ellis doing here?'

'The last time I heard, he was in London,' Melanie said. 'Maybe he came to see me, I rang him several times but he was always away.'

Jamie's head turned sharply. 'You rang him? Why?'

She looked at him with a placatory smile. 'I still haven't managed to give him back that ring, and it's worth a fortune—just having it in the house makes me nervous in case I lose it or we're burgled.'

Jamie relaxed. 'Oh, I see.'

She slid out of the car and walked with him up to the front door. Aunt Dolly met them in the hall, very flushed and agitated. She didn't notice Jamie, she was so disturbed by the news she had to give Melanie.

'Melanie, Ross is here! I didn't know what to say to him, I was so embarrassed! He's in the sitting-room, with Liz. She didn't want to talk to him, either, but one of us had to! Thank heavens you're home. Go and see what he wants.' She pushed Melanie towards the door. 'Oh, when I saw him outside I nearly dropped through the floor. I'm too old for these upsets.'

That was when she saw Jamie and stopped talking, her jaw dropping.

He smiled at her with all his considerable charm. 'Hallo, Mrs Nesbitt.'

Melanie didn't wait to hear him twining Aunt Dolly round his little finger; she pushed open the sitting-room door and Liz and Ross spun to look at her, their faces flushed.

She wasn't sure what she had interrupted—a quarrel or a very intimate talk. What she did realise was that neither of them was thrilled to see her.

'I'm glad you're here, Ross,' she said politely. 'I wanted to make sure you got your ring back safely, that was why I rang. I'll run upstairs and get it for you.'

She backed out before he could answer and closed the door again. She had never felt so unwanted in her life. There was no sign of Jamie but she heard voices in the kitchen and picked out his, smiling. Aunt Dolly was laughing. No doubt she had been a pushover for him. Aunt Dolly liked men, especially attractive ones.

Melanie didn't hurry back with the ring. She took the opportunity of changing into something rather more alluring while she was in her bedroom, and was just doing her make-up when Liz tapped on the door and put her head round it.

Melanie grinned at her. 'I was just coming down. You haven't murdered Ross, have you?'

Liz was still flushed but her eyes were bright and she was smiling. 'Not yet, but I still may.' She paused, then said uncertainly, 'Melanie, if I went out with him would it bother you? He just asked me to have dinner and I . . .'

'Idiot,' Melanie said fondly. 'Why should it bother me? I told you, it was all a big mistake, Ross and me. We both realised it in time, thank heavens.' She ran the brush over her hair, watching

Liz in the mirror. 'Anyway, I'm having dinner with Jamie, and don't suggest a foursome because I want him all to myself.'

Liz didn't seem surprised by the news, she looked amused, in fact. 'Jamie said . . .' she began and then stopped.

Melanie swung on the dressing-table stool, eyeing her suspiciously. 'What did Jamie say?'

Liz laughed. 'That he fancied you and thought you fancied him,' she said, and Melanie gave her a cross look.

'He's too sure of himself by half!'

'Aren't all men?' Liz said drily. 'On the surface, anyway. That's their ego; they're so scared of losing face that they make a big thing of being totally confident whatever happens.'

Melanie listened with a mixture of amusement and realisation. It had never occurred to her before that Jamie might not be as assured as he seemed, or that he might be vulnerable too. She nodded slowly, getting up. Collecting the box which held the sapphire ring, she slid a hand through Liz's arm, smiling at her cousin.

'We'd better go down and join our men,' she said.

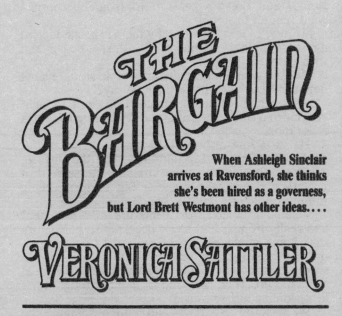

ATTRACTIVE, SPACE SAVING BOOK RACK

Display your most prized novels on this handsome and sturdy book rack. The hand-rubbed walnut finish will blend into your library decor with quiet elegance, providing a practical organizer for your favorite hard-or soft-covered books.

Only $9.95

Approximately 16" x 8" when assembled

Assembles in seconds!

To order, rush your name, address and zip code, along with a check or money order for $10.70* ($9.95 plus 75¢ postage and handling) payable to *Harlequin Reader Service*:

Harlequin Reader Service
Book Rack Offer
901 Fuhrmann Blvd.
P.O. Box 1396
Buffalo, NY 14269-1396

Offer not available in Canada.

BKR-1A

*New York and Iowa residents add appropriate sales tax.

Harlequin Presents

Coming Next Month

Available in December wherever paperback books are sold, or through Harlequin Reader Service:

In the U.S.
901 Fuhrmann Blvd.
P.O. Box 1397
Buffalo, N.Y. 14240-1397

In Canada
P.O. Box 603
Fort Erie, Ontario
L2A 5X3

**For the millions who can't read
Give the Gift of Literacy**

One out of five adults in North America
cannot read or write well enough
to fill out a job application
or understand the directions on a bottle of medicine.

**You can change all this by joining the fight
against illiteracy.**

For more information write to:
Contact, Box 81826, Lincoln, Neb. 68501
In the United States, call toll free: 1-800-228-8813

**The only degree you need
is a degree of caring**